The FAR REACH

To GERRI,

THANK YOU FOR REACHING
FAR INTO OUR LIFE'S
LEGACY!

ENJOY!

The FAR REACH

DAVID MUELLER

ARCHWAY
PUBLISHING

Archway Publishing books may be ordered through booksellers or by contacting:

Archway Publishing
1663 Liberty Drive
Bloomington, IN 47403
www.archwaypublishing.com
1 (888) 242-5904

Scripture quotations taken from The Holy Bible, New International
Version® NIV® Copyright © 1973 1978 1984 2011 by Biblica,
Inc. TM. Used by permission. All rights reserved worldwide.

ISBN: 978-1-4808-8482-3 (sc)
ISBN: 978-1-4808-8483-0 (hc)
ISBN: 978-1-4808-8484-7 (e)

Library of Congress Control Number: 2019920688

Print information available on the last page.

Archway Publishing rev. date: 12/31/2019

In dedication to

Karen,

my Kami,
and a gift to my father
and my daughter.

A *journey is a person in itself; no two are alike.*
And all plans, safeguards, policing, and coercion are
fruitless. We find that after years of struggle that we do not take a
trip; a trip takes us.

—John Steinbeck

*T*his is a novel written through the author's transformational experiences. It is meant for enjoyment. Nothing in it should be construed to offend or promote anything. A part of it is realized. A part of it is creative. A part of it is experienced. Most parts inspired by truth. The names are merely illustrative in nature. If you should find a liking to yourself in any of it, it is neither representational nor factual. If anything, it should beckon one's attention to read on, as only any writer would wish for his book.

PREFACE

*T*o be brief, everyone has a book in them. Whether written or not, it still exists in the shape of our lives. Rarely does our journey in life move in a straight line from beginning to end. We all encounter proverbial bumps along the way. I am no different.

This fictional read parallels two lives at different times. It is punctuated by intergenerational impacts at pivotal moments that steer the story. Often it directs to re-center or begin another trajectory in the characters' realm. It allows tensional introspection at times. The aim is to present the creative nature of a revealing composition.

It has been said that every writer uncovers an insight into a broader journey. As it matters to the reader, I hope this book conceptualizes that understanding. Some will perceive this fictional literacy as a learning experience toward a greater truth. Some may see obscure passages expressed in unexpected adventures. My intent is to cajole and imperceptibly draw the reader into the novel.

As with fine wine, the season of fermentation and uninterrupted aging favors a distinctive taste. In a similar fashion, this work has incubated in me for some time. Surfaced through a Japanese experience, I reflected on its personal meaning. It allowed a story to unfold, un-perceptively stream through me, and exit upon these pages. If it has any merit, this novel will beckon the reader to go further at every moment.

I am grateful for this un-pressed time to write. No doubt, it has spirited an awakening in myself. Hopefully, it will inspire the reader's own story.

If it prevails, everyone has a book in them.

Enjoy.

I

He stepped onto the tarmac. This day had been a long time coming. To finally be home is the soldier's ultimate triumph. But his experiences would not leave him for a while, for his homecoming was clouded by uncertainties that remained from his time spent in Japan.

TJ had sent many letters home. Each described his toilsome odyssey across the late summer storming Pacific. Now, the salty ocean air was replaced by the yeasty malt smells of the old brew town he grew up in. In later years he would often remark to his compatriot Art, "In all that time, what I wouldn't have given for a Pabst Blue Ribbon beer."

The great Lake Michigan lay within his view, taking him back to the swimming days of his youth and then, in contrast, to the Sea of Japan. His carefree swimming as a kid differed from the desperate venture of the Nippon backstroke boys out from the mainland, each hoping to hitch a ride to the New World on a U.S. warship cruiser. He remembered seeing bobbing bodies gasping and calling in broken English, "America, take me with you." In all that time, he could think only of his homeland. It made dropping off the young Japanese at the next row island all the easier.

The Pacific Crossing was not without peril. The temper of the ocean at that tropical time of year was ominous. One did all he could to stay dry, warm, and level to the horizon. TJ and his mates would only recall the upheaval in their stomachs during this voyage. They were encased in a floating bottle bobbing and tossing every which way. When the cruiser made the great push for Los Angeles landfall, they found the Baja waterway to the south calmer and preferable. The seasonal migration of giant gray whales led them to a descent below Baja. It would be the only tranquil, warm blue waters and aquatic grazing grounds they would experience. Their reentry into America was just delayed by their passage through the grand canal of Panama.

The crew welcomed the thumb-sized mosquitoes in the canal as a relief to the past month of relentless sea-swept stomachaches. The narrows of Panama belched into the waters of the Gulf of Mexico. Hurriedly, they swerved tightly around the panhandle of Florida, then it was full throttle north along the Atlantic coast into the welcomed sea lane ending at Norfolk naval base. All the while TJ thought to himself incessantly, "I never thought I would navigate around America. I just want to be back in it." Finally, he boarded the designated army transit plane for Milwaukee.

It was the lieutenant's return to his beloved hometown. Yet, in disembarking the plane, he was acutely aware that something was different. The ticker tape and cheers were out of sight and sound. The folks and his sweetheart knew the arrival time; it had been expressed and updated frequently in a handful of letters. Nonetheless, he observed an eerie quiet as he entered the terminal.

Hence, he sat and waited in his clean and pressed officer's uniform. Waited and waited at Billy Mitchell Field. His bag and victory trunk tucked firmly between his legs, as if somehow he could lose them now. He began to perseverate. His mind obsessed. How unfittingly late the welcome party was in traveling six miles compared to a returning son's journey of six thousand. "Really," he sighed. It was like to what he had become accustomed to on the prefecture of Kyushu.

"How could they understand," he muttered under his breath. With a withdrawn facial pout, he closed his eyes. He took solace in the words he recalled from his late command under MacArthur: "Old soldiers never die, they just fade away." Exhausted, he dozed off into dreams of a faraway reach.

TJ was one of two hundred thousand troops in steel-clad flotillas staggered throughout the chessboard Japanese island rims. As a commanding officer, he used pithy words of battle such as, "Boys, we're going to take the mainland of Japan, but rest assured, they will throw everything at us ... including the kitchen sink." As he spoke, he became known among his men for his trite fetching style. He believed somehow it would reassure them, especially when paired with his characteristic smirking grin. His primary role was to exemplify the esprit de corps. Although he made them ready for anything, in 1945, *anything* would not include the atomic surprise awaiting.

Like most officers, TJ was educated about imperialism. What he learned of Japan's military culture in aggression disprized his ardent beliefs in humanity. He enlisted while in college and was rewarded rank as first lieutenant in the United States Marine Corp Second Division Pacific Rim. In 1943, his active duty boot camp began at Great Lakes Naval Academy just outside Chicago. Thereafter he welcomed his commissioned officer training in California. There he met up with his good friend, Art, from elementary school.

Initially, TJ and Art had wanted to join the Navy. After all, the dapper white chaps and sharp attire was enviable, besides the turned gaze from any woman. Best of all, they would be together. Nothing like old friendship and lighthearted conversation between two homies. But the Navy would not have it for TJ. He would have had to surrender some of his rank to be a part of that team. The Marines were hungrier to have him at that time. They offered more in the arena of decorated favor and Marine life decorum. As a commissioned first lieutenant, he could commandeer the helm of a PT-109. After all, he grew up around water and loved operating boats. He remembered waxing his dad's mahogany-grained speedboat. He welcomed the opportunity to hone his navigation maneuvers as he had around the lily pads of Wisconsin lakes.

However, in ship life, when necessary, there was little doubt that all hands joined the effort to swab the decks and polish the rails from stern to bow. As he waited for his commands, he was reminded of the patience needed to develop his expertise in a wartime environment. Every night he consciously rehearsed what was expected of his leadership skills. He was banking on his beach training at Camp Pendleton, California to prepare him for the shores of the rising sun.

Franklin Roosevelt orchestrated the strategy for victory in the Pacific. Although the Marines' dutiful allegiance at sea was to MacArthur, the future of Washington, D.C. had other things in mind. The testing of a new weapon showed promise in the desert lands of New Mexico and Nevada, so the new President Truman hurried to move it into the war arena quickly. He felt that America was at its peak potential for resolving conflicts as Allied Russia began to see its vision expanding. The evolution of political wills was tethered on the fringes: One fell in with democracy and the other with communism. MacArthur saw his marshaling role in banishing any red completely.

TJ could read the concern on the face of the commander general, whose experiences in South Asia benefited him with unique strategic alliances and moves. However, Washington, D.C. was signaling a different path. Since the surrender of the Germans, Truman was anxious to wrap things up, while MacArthur was more patient in taking Japan. After all, he had lived a great number of years in the Asian Pacific area and understood the local cultures. He spoke quite frequently to his men about the history of the emperors, shoguns, and samurai working in unison to modernize the islands since the 1900s. He knew of Japan's great ambition to cover the Earth with the roof of divinely inspired imperialism. Though elusive, the metaphorical Russian bear hid patiently, waiting to take a swipe at Korea and Japan as it became opportune. This knowledge weighed deeply on the president's decision making.

TJ remembered MacArthur saying, "The trick card has already been played by the Soviets. They know Japan is within their reach. It is just a matter of time. But we are ready and prepared to act."

TJ wondered about the rush to preparedness which began in August of 1945. He knew that at any moment, his number and crew would be called upon. The men were called on deck early one morning to witness a new development forty-five degrees off starboard. They were asked to focus their eyes in the direction of the horizon. It was announced that if it was successful, the crew's mission would involve the repatriation phase of the enemy. At the moment, TJ did not understand the implications of this news, nor what it entailed.

The view was clear and quiet when the atomic bomb detonated. Where he was standing, it blinked blindly in the flash of an eye. The rise of dark cloudy ash fit the size of his thumb elongated at arm's reach. Beside him Art wondered aloud, "Is this the usual weather pattern interacting with Pacific trade winds?" No one had any idea that this spectacle was over a densely populated area. As murmurs cycled, an announcement was made via the speaker system on deck. The first atomic weapon in history had been used. Hopefully, it would hasten surrender of the conflict. All they could do now was wait and see what was next.

To pass the time, TJ played a card game called Sheepshead with his men. It was a Milwaukee deck game that involved a poker-like stance with two against one or three against two for the best hand to take a trick. It reminded him of the resolve to win, lose, or play it out regardless of outcome. A lot of nickels and cigarettes exchanged hands over the next six days.

Anxious about the news, TJ and Art wrote letters back home. A new secret weapon could bring them home early. Little did they know that home was better informed than they were at sea. Although they had firsthand visuals at a safe distance to the explosive phenomena, they began to grip themselves for comprehending the results and expectations to come.

TJ and Art were prepped for landfall in the machine arms production area in the Kyushu prefecture of Japan. They knew now that Hiroshima had been leveled. Kokura was a serious target, as it was deemed the steel-making center for warships and submarines. They coursed the cruiser in that direction. However, a murkiness obscured their view from afar. A second muted flash was observed southwest of Kokura, followed by a darkened cloud rising from the sea. Because of the mist and haze, it seemed directionally inconclusive. Moments later, the ship's loudspeaker confirmed that the drop called "Fat Man" had destroyed the city of Nagasaki. It was now apparent that Japan had few options.

Somehow sadness and relief played simultaneously in the minds of the crew. Art mused solemnly, "What is it about mankind that we resort to the cruelty of destruction when an answer cannot be found?" The officers and men removed their hats and caps as if they desperately wished for a conclusive answer. TJ smarted, "They started it!" and the crew echoed his words. Art replied, "Exactly my point!"

The rest of the day was deathly quiet. Orders came in to head into the eastern bay of Tokyo. Japan had surrendered.

They were still a long distance away from the mainland of Japan, known as Honshu. The smaller islands scattered and dotted in a line south, showing their distinctive stark, rocky faces to the ocean. It would be a strategic place for resistive enemy forces to hide and strike out from. Most of Japan was known for its rural mountainous sweeps. The undeveloped rugged terrain made up about seventy percent of the country. It was only in the flat areas surrounding the estuaries that the dense population resided.

The seat of growth and modernization was Tokyo, named Edo by the locals. In the nineteenth century, feudal families and shoguns shared their lands and military might for the protection of the eternalized emperor. It was only when a centralized government was necessary for the entire Japanese islands that Edo developed into the center seat, reflecting the forward thinking of the emperor. The late Emperor Meiji was challenged to keep Japan's imperial and independent position. In Japan's developing psyche, one could not forget the role of Commodore Perry's display of full white blanket sails rising on floating albatrosses outside the bay. Change was coming, and Japan could not keep its doors shut for much longer. The emperor struck fear in the populace by promulgating stories of human-shaped sea serpents that threatened to pillage their people, riches, and landscapes. Up until then, protective typhoons kept sacred Japan's peoples, warding off invasion and wreaking havoc all the way back to Genghis Khan; truly, nature's destructive fury was praised as a godsend to the natives. In the past, it had crashed many a hostile vessel. But the Japanese could no more rely on its catastrophic strength against the ingenuity of human inventions.

A flotilla of United States battleships came to a halt about fifty miles from an estuary bay. The official surrender was to be performed at sea. Art pointed out, "This is just like the Japanese. They still have the imperialistic myth that the emperor is God, and that God can never surrender, especially in His Garden of Eden." He sighed. "I wonder if they truly believe they have surrendered, or ever even would."

TJ confidently reassured him, "They did surrender. Otherwise, they would all be dead. It is in their character and conduct. They are not to return to their soil without both intact. To not be victorious is not an option. It counters their belief of the divinity descendance of the empire and emperor of Japan. Thus, without faith and understanding, they can only surrender away at sea."

As the huddle of ships approached, they could see a single Japanese flag flying off a ship's stern amongst the plethora of American flags in the battleship brigade.

TJ commented, "That red circle on the white background. I wonder what it truly means."

A nearby Native American code talker overheard and replied, "It is the sun. A powerful sign for this country. The ancients believed the sun goddess is an ancestor of the emperor. That is what brings him power. They say the emperor is the son of the sun. It has been this way always. It has never changed. The sun surrenders to no one. It rises and sets of its own accord."

Art exclaimed, "Well, the sun is orange, and their sun is bloody red!"

The code talker spoke up once more. "For the Japanese, that crimson red represents prosperity for Japan. The white symbolizes the honesty, integrity, and purity of its people."

They looked on as the documented signatures on giant-sized tablets were ceremoniously performed. It was as if a clean sweep of history prevailed. Complete submission and humility were in order. Post signing, the nation's flag and its held significance were banished throughout Japan as a contentious symbol of aggression and imperialism.

TJ and his men were given an unexpected furlough. Little did they realize that the un-pulled triggers and bayonets in their weaponry would be substituted for sticks and shovels. He remembered MacArthur's speech: "Men, we are ready for a new phase of humanity in the rebuilding of a new social democracy unlike ours, similar in improvement, yet prosperous beyond what we know."

First, they had to survey the new field. TJ took his marine crew and Art his naval troops. They parted from their rendezvous at sea with good wishes. TJ embarked with a dozen men in his grand motorboat. It was a torpedo boat, better known as a PT-109. The Japanese civilians called them mosquito boats on water. They carried a stinger in the tubular torpedo chamber. The lieutenant was accompanied by a line of others and a well-equipped cruiser. They were destined for the obscure port of Sasebo on the island of Kyushu.

Finding a port to dock at was not an easy task. TJ could not help but notice the rows of small boats facing the sea. It was if they were lined up in a poll position at the beginning of a stock boat race. As the Americans closed in, they saw that many were outfitted with ropes and cradles, as if to carry some load strapped to the hull. TJ had a code talker on board equipped for translation. However, the nuances of local symbolisms and signs were mystifying. He radioed for an English-speaking Japanese scout that would give him the lay of the land.

He slowed the boat for transit under a huge orange lacquered gate with a hand-notched winged crossbeam overhead. It stood unfettered in the channel of water. On the shoreline, he got a glimpse of a structure shrouded in trees and bamboo. A slate roof feathered up to the sky as if ready to catch the breeze and take flight. It was deathly quiet. He had not expected to beach without inhabitants in view. He throttled back slowly and deliberately. He expected anything, knowing that imperial news might travel slower here. As he started to reach shallow sand, he recalled his beach dune training at California's Camp Pendleton, though quite dissimilar a shore. The higher terrain and surrounding mountain caves could harbor firepower, and attack could very well commence at will.

The men had orders to disembark and scout around. The lieutenant sat back for a moment and settled into the captain's seat, removing his aviator glasses. He was familiar now with the ease of his boat and comfortable on the water. He had not yet stepped on foreign soil up to this point. He looked down to pull the key out from the ignition and noticed that it had the California state emblem dangling from its ring. He held it and paused momentarily. He sighed, then sat back again into the deep cushioned seat. He was alone on the boat for the first time. He shut his eyes and projected back to the previous beach he had set boots on ... Oceanside, California.

II

TJ's first real trip out of Wauwatosa, Wisconsin was through the Marines. He felt that the brief enlistment phase in backyard Chicago, a mere seventy miles away from home, did not count. He was going to California. The excitement of the year-round pleasant temperatures, palm trees, and glamourous repute of the area enticed him. Having his high school friend, Art, heading in that direction as well made the move even easier. They stayed close; Art was stationed seaside in San Diego while TJ's residence was to be just north of Carlsbad. The Milwaukee winters were what they looked forward to leaving the most—it claimed the best excuse in getting away from the unending shoveling of snow. Of course, they were sad to deal with the emotions of family and sweethearts wishing them off. Nonetheless, they saw it as a new, unprecedented life chapter much less than an exciting adventure. They answered the country's call and wholeheartedly joined in on the termination of the imperialistic aggressors.

TJ's brother felt no different, nor did his sister. His brother, Richard, took to the sky with the air force. He welcomed the challenges of Alaska's training grounds. After all, it was the last frontier. Where else could you be a hero and ruff explorer? His sister, Betts, discovered her duty in advocating for the troops at home. In the factories, she geared up to the "sister riveter" motto. The call of duty to one's country had little to do with abilities except to do one's part.

From the moment he landed in California and breathed in the ocean air, he was sold. In his writings, he quoted it as his "golden times." He engaged in every bit of it. As an officer in the Marines, he was spared no training on the beach. The rigorous exercises of confrontational and self-defense skills with and without weapons were diligently practiced. He even learned how to throw sand as an excellent deterrent. Climbing rope, tire running, and push-ups fostered his long-time habit of fitness. As in his youth, his natural aptitude lay foremost in beach running. To a lesser degree, his domestic skills as in bed tidiness, garment pressing, and hygiene were a reminder of his mother's teachings, only to be reinforced by the Marines. The daily sweat and late-night officer manual reading hastened relief in good night sleeps. His golden behavior was checked on weekend leaves, beginning with ocean surfing, a cooler of cold lagers, and sand volleyball.

The first weekend was an unexpected one. Art drove up for a visit. He came by in a convertible with two girls and surprised TJ with an agenda. "TJ, jump in. We're headed to the beach." This was characteristic of the bon vivant and charming nature of his friend. When TJ inquired how he had gotten the car, Art responded, "I didn't, it belongs to her! Now get in!"

TJ's biggest distraction was the provincial Southern California attire. He often would reflect to Art, "How do these locals drive cars without shoes on? In Milwaukee this would not go! Is it legal?" Art would reassure him, "TJ, relax ... We're in Cali." Much ado about nothing; he got used to the sand between his toes and would later consider it not a bad price to pay. Hence was founded TJ and Art's shared relish for the California lifestyle and freedom.

Despite the reality of the war, it seemed an innocently sought-out relief to delay the looming end of the party. TJ had to remind himself to stay focused because the war was the reason he was here. But he soon learned that leisure time was imperative to the ability to withstand the upcoming stresses.

TJ was to become an officer, which meant troops at his command. His testing was strict and thorough. He was called to exhibit tactical aqua motoring skills to safely maneuver into positioning during engagement. Fellow officers coined the nickname "the Wisconsin lakes wizard" for the lieutenant's natural proclivities on water. He deftly avoided subsurface torpedo lanes as set up in mock runs. However, in other practices, his instincts served him not. He shunned the instruments to guide him around what he failed to see. When he clipped three fake mines on one run, the instructor utilized him as an example. "Boys, you may know your feel and skill. But don't deny these boats their technical prowess to detect disaster. You must master all aspects of your craft in order to anticipate and stay ahead." In the Marines, humbling lessons were built in to guarantee subsequent success and mission safety. Later on, TJ found a message taped to his locker. It read: *It is always better to fail here NOW than when you leave as a MARINE.*

He wrote home on weekends. He spoke of his training and how much he was learning. He missed his family, his girl, and his friends in the Midwest. He even wrote a letter to his dog Blackie. How he would enjoy a beachfront run here. He mentioned Art. How he took the time on leave to travel up to Oceanside. Always willing to support TJ and expose him to the best of what California offered.

He wrote, *On one occasion, Art's "top-down car acquaintances"—as they became to be known—drove us to MGM Studios for a look at Hollywood's playground. It was swell. We were introduced to actors Ronald Reagan and Doris Day. Not long after, we were introduced to Louis B. Mayer of MGM. He made a promise* to us cadets: *"When the war is over, come back and jobs will be waiting for you at the studios!"*

TJ even received a late letter from his brother in Alaska. Richard enjoyed the grand landscape of the wilderness and commented that he might end up staying there after his service. His training included flying over the Aleutian Islands with the air force. He mentioned locating the presence of the Japanese bases there. The hurried construction of the ALCAN Highway for supplies and reinforcements was paramount. Unsurprised by the mock stations across the Bering Strait, he conjectured, *They must have feared waking the Russian bear to the northwest!* At the end of the letter he asked TJ, *You plan to stay in California when this is all done?* TJ wrote back, *I do enjoy it, but the folks back home will probably not approve.* Richard came back with, *TJ, I get it with Pop's, but heck! Isn't it something?* He then followed, *Oh, and I met a great gal from California. They tend to breed them there!* TJ chuckled and stuffed the letter in his top buttoned pocket for future reference.

Art came up from San Diego to share the news that he got his orders for shipping out. TJ asked him, "Where to?"

"An island they call Naha," Art responded. "They are holding a fortification called Okinawa there. Hell, it's a thousand miles away from the Jap mainland. What good is that?" He continued, "I'd rather head down to Mexico with the army to reinforce a shipping channel and roadway through a small fishing village there. I hear the fishing, margaritas, and mujeres are great!"

"Oh Art," TJ exclaimed, "that sounds too mischievous, and you'd get bored."

"Try me!" He shook TJ's hand and said, "Mañana, soldier!"

The lieutenant's own itinerary was not as clear. It was relayed to the men at base camp that the First Division Marines were preparing the way. A landing force in coordination with the navy began strikes in the southern islands of Japan. The orders were to work their way up to mainland as reinforcements. They were now entering the second phase of the war strategy.

TJ knew where his Second Division would be called upon to steer the march toward complete victory. But he also knew through his training that the Japanese had never before been invaded on this scale. They would hunker down in whatever capacity necessary to keep the American flag from waving over their heads. He had hoped he would parallel the navy with Art again; yet, his duty was to go where needed. The recent Battle of Midway had turned the tide and regressed the aggressors onto their heels. It was the momentum they had been looking for.

The orders came to ship out. "Semper Fidelis" was the code word. They departed from the Southern California port. TJ stared at America until land no more could be seen, all too aware that he might never step on his native soil again.

III

Reports were coming in as TJ's Second Division set out to sea. The ocean lanes were calm. But the Japanese were known for surprise. The Australian allies were stationed along the lanes for support in the Pacific crossing sea channels. But it was the area intersecting lanes where straggler surface mines and submarines darted about, and it was here that TJ's previously exhibited skills were called upon.

Instead of cruisers and battleships, it was destroyers and swift torpedo boats being deployed to navigate ahead in order to counter any potential disturbances to the mission. Normally, the destroyers could pick up a pin drop in any of the high seas. An enemy submarine would bow in and out of the sea lanes at a far distance, so as not to be detected. This was where the PT-109 could create a perimeter band. Its characteristic swift sizing and navigational ability to warn, interrupt, and deter the route of metallic mirrors at water's surface was legendary. Besides, submarines were not to waste any time with pesky "mosquito boats" when bigger bats were on deck. By now, the Japanese strategy was well known:

They put up with the "fly swatting" to save the punch for the big score, even at the cost of a counter torpedo.

It was then that TJ set out with half his crew to survey the waters around. Fortunately, the seas reminded him of the mildly choppy days on the lakes back home. He swiftly made time around the fleet. In fact, he began to stopwatch himself for best times. When the repetition bored him, he made for a new, more interesting chapter in the manual by increasing his perimeter. That way he could improve efficiencies for fewer numbers of PT-109s to be deployed in the convoy. Of course he logged it all. As an officer, he believed he was setting a new standard of torpedo boat operation that would bear his name among future surveillance brigades.

Then the unthinkable happened. Something not even in the manual he had absorbed since his first rebuke in training. He considered it almost an act of God. A Japanese submarine surfaced a hundred yards away, between his craft and the rest of the brigade. In quasi-shock TJ mumbled, "How could this be? How could he not see me, and how could I miss this on my radar screen?" It seemed a path had been woven to direct sonar away from each other. He immediately knew that the sub was trying to position a good look at a certain target of choice. TJ gestured to hush his men. His aim was to surprise the sub on its blind side. He prayed the above-head hatch would open for just a look. Just the same, he positioned the torpedo bay for deployment.

As he hoped, the steel chamber door creaked in the salt water as the vertical hatch opened. A head popped out with a set of binoculars as if to sight a lucky prize. Unbelievably, another completely climbed out to take a quick relief off the side of a turret.

TJ gave the sign, and the spark of twin M2 .50-cal machine guns blazed. His first mate shouted, "Sir, shall we deploy the Mark 8 torpedo?" TJ put his hand down to wait. The submarine closed its hatch with only half the man from the turret inside and immediately dived. TJ remarked, "Well, I believe we caused enough excitement to last a lifetime for the kids in the tin bucket today." His crew laughed and cheered. It was their first experience of combat. They made their way back to the convoy.

Fortunately, no one noticed the shaking of TJ's hands. After that encounter, he turned in his report at captain's quarters in the brigade. He was complimented on a job well done. He finally comprehended that any failure was not to be tolerated at any expense.

The group stayed tight as they cleared shipping lanes. Uneventful navigation was the goal. The scope was to bring the naval fleets reinforcements of arms, food, supplies, and additional manpower. It was apparent that the seas were indeed clearing, except for maybe a few drifting renegade crafts. They had been out to sea so long they fished now for survival. As the battalion approached Guam, they signaled with provisions and declared a quiet night's sleep. It was in the morning they would refuel and resume a course toward Okinawa. It was April 1, 1945 and the crew heard that the First Division was still battling on the "peep" island, still far off from the mainland.

On Guam, TJ got a read from the *Pacific Daily News* under the headline, "Okinawa struggle not letting up." Only afterwards, he found it to be the largest marine amphibious assault in the Pacific Rim. They had another thousand miles to go to the site of battle. Fortunately, the seas were smooth and the fight was concentrated there. They slowed to a halt ten miles away from the fighting. They could see and smell the smoke of gunnery and cannon fire off the battleships. Air support from the aircraft carriers was relentless. The marines positioned themselves in cattle car-like formation to deploy at the shoreline. Throughout the night, they heard the rat-a-tat at all hours over the stained ocean surface.

TJ and his division were at sea there for twenty-two days supplying his First Division comrades. The exhausted battle of 50,000 troops against 120,000 ended with the historic rise of the first American flag on Japanese turf. It was all in the struggle to capture and claim a strategic piece of rock.

TJ witnessed deckside the first foreign claim to a battle cry. One First Division returnee described them: "An enemy totally surrounded, without desire to give up or to surrender." It was almost like in the playbook. The Japanese would resort to the island caves in order to slip back out and fight again. It was apparent that the flushing out with flamethrowers and hand grenades deterred them not. The few wounded prisoners who were taken had not the means to take their own lives. The conflict became known as Operation Downfall.

Upon later reflection on these days, the lieutenant recalled no claim to cheer or celebrate. Care for the wounded, cleanup, and burials were in order for both sides. He stood still as the First Division took the charge, thinking only of what might be next for his Second. Suddenly, he heard a voice shout, "TJ!" and he looked up. It was his friend Art. They grabbed each other's forearms, glued to the creases in each other's eyes. Neither of them spoke.

It was apparent that General MacArthur was on the march to assure the men of pressing victory. The map was clear, showing the plethora of islands to be taken. However, the jagged rockiness and innumerable hideouts of the slopes of these small, likely inhabited islands was a sure sign of the ensuing crawl to take place.

At this time Okinawa became the boxing ring where Truman and MacArthur would trade jabs on the ultimate strategy to adopt. One man the president, commander in chief of the United States in Washington, D.C.; the other commander and field marshal in the Pacific arena. They were seven thousand miles apart. The marines, along with the navy and army troops, converged offshore here and waited patiently. The number gathered in this area was 275,000 now. They heard Operation Olympic, with the purpose of taking the homeland, was about to begin but no clues were given as to what exactly was to commence. They knew it would be unlike what they had heard about in the European corridor. It was apparent the fate of this divinely inspired nation would fall to the desperate acts of the kamikaze.

Art remarked in the mess hall, "They will stop at nothing, not even for a last cigarette." TJ reluctantly followed, "It is not in their nature, Art," and paused. " ...Well, it's a new month. Maybe August will be better."

IV

The lieutenant was startled and awoke disoriented in his seat. A private had appeared to summon him: "Lieutenant, sir, we have a way into Sasebo. You need to take a look." TJ sat up from the wheel, took the keys from the switch, and straightened his officer's hat.

They went up a bending hill around a grove of cherry blossom trees. The terrain turned to dense evergreens, then to giant red pines as they wound their path through the forested island. At the top point of the mesa, the private pointed out toward the sea inlet. In the harbor channel, dozens of glistening Nippon light cruisers lay idle in neat rows. With binoculars, it set a picturesque scene of a sleek metal brigade nestled in slumber at bay.

"What is the command, sir?" the private asked.

The lieutenant relied on his training as he resolved, "We will hold our ground for now—until we have our scout." He had a crew code talker, but in this tenuous case, he felt a more local aide would serve as well.

The lieutenant was concerned. Since the official surrender off

Tokyo Bay, it was not as certain whether the more militarily industrial western end of Kyushu had promptly conceded. In fact, even the USS Missouri was not immune from a sneak attack, provided the number of dignitaries on board, if Japan were to try for one last treacherous act. Fortunately, it was not to be, as the emperor's word was considered divine.

TJ recruited the code talker, Private Yaz, and a captured English-speaking Japanese soldier named Takamatsu for interpreting the local situation at Sasebo. Takamatsu described at length the role of this nucleus of the imperial navy found in the harbor. Prior to surrender, these cruisers had been in operation to flag and ward off any prowling Russian fleets. They had all been abandoned now. However, as the Japanese spoke, the lieutenant found himself growing suspicious of the stories.

Finally, the lieutenant decided. A strategic roundup would occur. He would test the faith of the surrender by borrowing a page from MacArthur's book. A cooperative construction phase in and outside of the new militarized zones would commence. Thus, Sasebo was to become a new base for the fleets of the Allies and a port for fueling, besides a source of construction materials which were required for the repatriation mission. He was ready to call in for reserves, though he was left with one daunting question: What was to be expected from the scattered Japanese soldiers?

With the cruisers harbored at bay, TJ requested command for more troops and supplies. The battalion offshore obliged. Systematically, 109s and light runners cautiously paraded in formation through the bay. Not a light cruiser budged. It seemed the surrender had indeed reached the far ends of the nation.

As they navigated toward the piers of the city, TJ noticed how the locals' small boats and skiffs were arranged with bows facing out to the sea. He wondered why they were standing as if at attention. He looked at the code talker and asked, "Why are these boats so nosed out in the narrows of the harbor?" Yaz shrugged with no answer and grabbed the Japanese soldier-translator, pushing him in front of the lieutenant. TJ looked at Takamatsu with distrust but repeated to him, "What do you know of the placement of these small boats here?"

The man responded expressionlessly, "They are ready for deployment in the name of the emperor."

"Do they know the emperor surrendered?"

"Yes, lieutenant." He added, "But *bushido* says, best conduct is practiced through the unsafe days of unsettled periods."

TJ paused for a minute, ready to reprimand, but then pondered his response. Finally he spoke assuredly. "What does that have to do with our victory now?"

Takamatsu spoke proudly. "If I may, sir, war and glory are only two sources of chivalry. We stand guard with several more."

The lieutenant excused him but summoned Yaz with further directions, nodding toward the translator. "Keep an eye on him."

PT-109s were known to beach up on the gravel sand. The order was to do so as the swift crafts made their entrance. The crew jumped out expecting an awkward greeting. Instead, the women and children made way for them, as if they had had no notice of the landing. Most of the women wore strange-looking wrapped serapes with wooden shoes clapping on the ground while the children wore oversized worn khaki fatigues that slid past their hands and feet. It could not be seen whether they had shoes, since most children walked on the extended lengths of clothing. A few older men looked on with unimpressed expressions.

The lieutenant requested the translator, "Takamatsu, you say is your name?" The other sharply bowed. The lieutenant obliged, "Where are the men?" The Japanese responded reservedly, "Looking for work." TJ replied, "Well, it will be your job to round up those who are here or in this area. They need to know their conduct, as you would say." He stared squarely at him and continued, "Also, we need to procure all the guns and weapons." The other bowed subserviently again.

TJ sent a dozen men with Takamatsu with these orders. He

knew that he had to exhibit control in order to dismantle any of the war production works, keep the riffraff at bay, and raise morale. A marine soon ran up to him and delivered a thin envelope from command. It read: *Set up or build a prison stat.*

Sasebo's war construction buildings were in plain sight. But their unsecure features provided many hiding places and caverns which could facilitate both above- and below-ground escape. TJ thought of initiating a tear-down of the hefty beams of the winged roof-type structures, including the wooded gates that marked paths to the many temples and shrines in the area. A secure fence line around the perimeter was drawn and the setup of a cot base camp was envisioned. Further plans would depend on the number of captured. The manpower would be key. Patiently, the lieutenant waited for his scouts and Takamatsu to report back.

TJ and his crewmen became concerned about the return of the scouts as the sun set. Finally, they returned with over two hundred local men in count. Most were disheveled and hungry. All of them postured lowered heads as if shamed.

The Americans began to realize that this part of Japan was mostly poor rural, with an abundance of tradesmen and rice farmers. The engine of war had little supervision outside their apprenticeship, ingenuity, and agricultural know-how. Most of the books and manuals gathered and brought to the lieutenant were in German. In his officer's training, TJ remembered reading about the skills trade between Germany and Japan in the early 1900s. It was a way for Japan to modernize off their lead. It was during the Meiji time, when the emperor believed that mainland intrusion was inevitable and thus chose to network with the greatest industrial power. Germany, heavy in the industrial edge, swapped with Japan for their agriculture and automation, each to complement the other country's need. It was confirmed when the lieutenant asked to know what other languages Takamatsu spoke. His reply: "We were taught Japanese and German in school. The emperor mandated it for the future of our country."

The lieutenant addressed the mass. "We will begin building a camp and quarantine the prisoners. We will use the tools of the industry here. All the men will be treated fairly. They will have food and clothing. However, they must give up their weapons."

The private scout by the name of Huggins signaled to the lieutenant. "Sir, we know where all the weapons are from the prisoners. We need Jeeps and a truck to gather them."

"Good work," the lieutenant responded.

Takamatsu then spoke up. "Lieutenant, sir, what will happen to our women and children?"

"We will have provisions for them. We will set up a store for them to supply the workers with food as well."

Takamatsu interrupted, "But where will they stay?"

TJ responded annoyed, "We will make sure they have housing. They can return to where they were living with their children."

In the morning, trucks and Jeeps arrived off the ships. Private Huggins orchestrated a number of soldiers to gather up the guns and weapons scattered throughout the area and in homes. The prisoners were gathered into file at attention for the lieutenant to speak briefly. Yaz interpreted the warning: "The penalty will be harsh if we don't retrieve all the weapons." The prisoners bowed in understanding and submission.

The first complaint came from Takamatsu. He stated that the shrines should not be disrupted, as they had great significance for the land and to the people. TJ played the protest cleverly: "Give me a better solution," he challenged. Takamatsu responded, "We have many building materials in the shipyards to fortify the needs of the camp. We can also machine and make whatever is necessary to have a solid structure. Many men are skilled in woodworking and welding. They prefer simple quarters with a futon for sleeping." The lieutenant responded, "I will inspect all materials and details for the construction. We will begin immediately."

The Marine crews were quick to observe the skill levels of the Japanese. The prisoners preferred not to use the glue or nails they were given. They were keen on notching wood with chisels and etching with squares. Their skills became more apparent to the foreigners. Each man would procure choice wood with drawn interlocking joints. A rubberized mallet was utilized to pound and angle wooden struts for a secure fit. A site map was provided with a squared-off perimeter. Personalized styles for rooms for housing and sleep were allowed, if the outdoor cots were not desired. However, the latter were actually preferred.

The precise craft making was remarkable to see. They sketched renditions of side supports and sloping roof lines. They managed water troughs from walking areas into drinking cisterns. It was quite detailed but simple in design. They not only possessed farming skills but construction design ability as well, particularly in complement to this environment. Within twelve hours, the drawings were reviewed and reconfigured to display a uniform building site. They even planned to weld a metal shed for arms storage and protection. It became apparent that the repatriation and rebuilding of Sasebo was an ambitious enterprise. Their emperor had prepared them well to usher in modernization at breakneck speed.

TJ decided that the first building to be completed would be a food mart. The locals had not yet been introduced to residential refrigeration, but the U.S. would be preparing them for consumerism. Besides, the Japanese had developed an affinity for certain American delights such as bubble gum, Coca Cola, and cigarettes. The experience of cold stocked dairy products, cold fizzy water, preserved seafood, and soba noodles turned their attention. However, they attempted American-style sandwiches and fast food without much gastronomic success.

Local fisherman came by and enticed the TJ's crew with food called sashimi. Blue fin tuna with rice, fresh caught from the sea. It was an instant hit with the Americans. Undoubtedly, their demonstration of superior skills with knives, proven by paper-thin cuts of meats and fish, made the soldiers only too wary of that style of personal confrontation.

Yet, for the prisoners, sticky rice, wasabi, water, and tea would suffice. For the locals, most successful was the all-hours food store. It was a good start.

The prisoners worked diligently from after sunrise to just before sundown. As the prison was erected to plan, wing-like colonnades extended beyond the canopies. They looked to serve no particular purpose except to simulate an image of a phoenix with feathers flowing elegantly along the rooftop. The prison was turning into a Japanese-style village. It could serve as a handsome quarter for some time—although, it was not certain how long they would be there. Yaz spewed, "It's becoming something like you find in *National Geographic!*"

The perimeter of the prison was complete within four days and the interior structures took fifteen. Only the outskirt was reinforced with wire. Even then, it was bored through timber holes without a kink. The local women made futons with burlap cloth and stuffed them with straw. It became a collaborative local effort to provide additional materials, resulting in homely features they were accustomed to.

The roof took two more weeks. The main quarter beams were delicately slanted and placed to catch rainwater and chain-link-drop the liquid into additional wooden cisterns. From there, they would drink or clean it with a sculpted wooden ladle. The lieutenant and his men observed all this. They were impressed by the collective cooperation and civility and the project's peaceful nature.

V

New orders came from command: Any guns and other weapons used for battle were to be collected, dismantled, and destroyed. TJ found this directive difficult to follow. He saw firsthand the locals' meticulous practice of their skilled trades. Upon inspection, most of their weaponry was handcrafted in Japan, superior even to German standards. It was well known that the Japanese were skilled in sword making. Many of the soldiers captured had customized blade engravings with ancestral gems embedded into the hilts, reminiscent of the ancient samurai *kanto*. Mindfully, the lieutenant delayed execution of the order as long as he could.

Finally, the day came. The confiscated weapons had to be removed from their secured storage. Next, the lieutenant had to dispose of the gunpowder reserves. He had no choice but to head to sea to do so. He requested that twenty prisoners load up and stack the goods in his PT-109. He called upon Privates Yaz and Huggins to accompany him, and the three set out into the bay with the worker inmates to give the goods and ammunition their proper "machine parts burial," as he called it. Three miles out to sea from the docks seemed adequate.

As they slowed the boat into a calm area, TJ instructed Yaz to have the men throw the weapons overboard. He thought the deed could be done quickly. However, an uprising was brewing. The prisoners squirmed uncomfortably under the request. Huggins and TJ pulled their Lugers from their holsters and pointed them at the prisoners who then cried, "No, no, no!" The lieutenant requested Yaz to explain their urge to disobey. The latter spoke with one of the men and immediately translated, "It is our fishing area. It will ruin our fishing." TJ and Huggins were somewhat relieved at this justification but continued holding out their arms. TJ told Yaz to ask where a better spot might be, and the prisoners interpreted silently with fingers pointing around a small island reef within sight.

TJ and Huggins kept their pistols pointed until they reached the destination. Only then did the prisoners pick up each weapon and toss it overboard, all the while sighing with disbelief. It was like tossing fine art into the fire. They began to murmur among themselves more forcefully and with disgust. Observing this, the officers kept a finger on the trigger. TJ noticed his hand trembling again. He looked at Huggins. They knew they were outnumbered. But further backlash was not demonstrated.

The crew and prisoners returned to the base. The dejected prisoners trudged back into the camp as if their sacred trademark of craftsmanship was insignificant. TJ went to his barrack and sat on his bed, his mind as unsteady as his still shaking hand. He had been ever so close to being stormed and himself becoming the goods tossed overboard. He thought back to the sparring between Truman and MacArthur regarding the next steps to take that early August after Okinawa. Superior orders from afar could never be taken lightly. They were often in contrast to the direct state of conditions in the field. Sometimes it felt all too unreal.

He lay back on his bed. He felt poking bars sticking up from the mattress below. It was then he recalled that between the boards and bedspring he kept a number of choice weapons. Like the many before him, to the victor belonged the spoils.

Every morning, before his run, he walked the perimeter of the camp. He noticed how neat and orderly the prisoners were. No trash was seen in any part of the grounds. He observed rake line patterns in the pitched white gravel. It seemed like secret code or perhaps an attempt to manicure the ground into some art form. Often, he would observe a mysterious ritual. The men would pour water over their hands with a spoon, then cup water into their mouths and spit it out. They would proceed to a perceived imaginary wall, clap their hands twice, and toss an open hand forward, as if delivering a coin into a fountain. With a step back, they would clasp their hands together as if in a silent chant of prayer. Finally, they would raise their head and clap hands once before walking away. It was a practice TJ observed multiple times a day. He asked Takamatsu what the meaning was. He replied, "Christians have their form of pray in church and at certain times. We have pray that you see, feel, and hear in our lives." He paused and then went on. "It is in the calling of our ancestors and deities that we heed along the journey. It is our path to wisdom, compassion, and understanding." TJ replied, "It sounds like a contorted religion of hedonism and idol worship to me. That is not the freedom that we bring to Japan!" Takamatsu respectfully ushered, "We will make further discussion another day."

Under the lieutenant's control, Sasebo was transforming into an installation base as planned. Command noticed and set focus on another area. He was to scope out nearby Kokura. The city was known for its mountains, historic castle, and harbor. It was larger and more sophisticated then Sasebo. Yaz would serve as his traveling interpreter.

TJ handed him the keys to a military star Jeep. Their map showed an approach through the high mountain forest. The vista of distant Korean islands on the horizon was impressive and the beaches below were uninhabited and pristine. Idle sheet metal factories with glistening stackers framed the panorama. Their destination city had a reputation as a workhorse for steel production.

In a peculiar way, he was grateful that Kokura was dubbed the "protected angel city." It had been the backup target during the atomic strikes on Hiroshima and Nagasaki. Cloud coverage had spared it. Somehow, it seemed fitting that TJ spent a day here since he, too, had been spared the strikes of battle. The two companions motored through the city without incident. At a downtown café, they tested the temperament of the population. They were served the locally popular ramen for the first time. It was so texturally tasty that they had another bowl, along with TJ's first taste of sake. The dining patrons raised ceramic cups and all toasted, *"Kanpai!"* The men had their fill and bowed to the hospitality at the end. For a moment, they thought to stay for a nightcap. Nonetheless, they returned so TJ could fill out his report.

The lieutenant was pleased to find Sasebo running smoothly. He began to notice a subtle coolness in the air. Snow was known to fall soon. The troops started to raise concerns about how much longer this stay would be. TJ addressed them with reassurance. "We are here building a democracy. It will be your hallmark in the call for freedom and diplomacy."

He did show positive regard for the morale of his men, primarily in his support for physical activity. Beach volleyball was new to these parts. The locals crowded around to witness the tossing and spiking of an inflatable ball to a purpose of questionable significance. Fish merchants and trinket stalls soon gathered around the makeshift court to support the interest of cheer in the burgeoning spectator sport.

Proverbially, afternoon naps were encouraged. The monsoons of moisture fostered a sweat with thirst to drink, cool off with a dip, and kick back in a hammock. However, on one occasion, the nap taking took a turn for the worse. First, security measures and threats were always patrolled. One day, TJ decided to check protocol with a stroll through the compound. To his chagrin, he found a guard asleep at a station. It was the only time TJ recalled losing his temper. He kicked the guard in the shin, spouting, "I can have you court-martialed for this!" Of course, the usual denial of resting the eyes was parlayed. Though he did not accept the excuse for the guard's lapse, in the end, the lieutenant decided not to pursue the matter.

Other days, he found some of the crew to appear scruffy and somewhat unkempt. From study of his officer's playbook, he knew regular routines would be prudent. The lieutenant instituted an early morning workout regimen with stretches and calisthenics. It was followed by a five-kilometer run. Invoking the spirit of the Camp Pendleton USMC training, he did callouts and callbacks during the routines. The exercises were rousing in the damp weather, tending to limber up the men. It also reminded the locals that the troops were in charge. Unquestionably, the mission of repatriation became modus operandi.

On one occasion, a celebrity arrived for an entertainment boost. The boys had heard of the USO and their spontaneous surprise tours, never revealing who would show. A Stateside-known comedian appeared onstage as a clown one afternoon at the base. To their delight, Danny Kaye fidgeted with amusing antics and attire, bringing the troops to raucous laughter. It was particularly timely, after the almost four months spent in Sasebo. A familiar face in a place that felt so far from home made their duty more palatable. Any such entertainment kept the secluded men content. Besides, it provided the locals another sample of strange American ways.

One thing TJ could not get over. His mind was still puzzled with the arrangement of the small local boats about the harbor entrance, as he had first noted upon his arrival. So he ordered Private Huggins to board one of the crafts. He would pay a local a stipend to take him to fish a mile offshore and he would be allowed to keep what they caught. Huggins, being an avid fisherman from the

Midwest, loved the idea. He boarded and took off with the local. The lieutenant observed through binoculars as, at half the distance out, the private suddenly ordered the boat be turned around, flashing his pistol. Upon docking, he revealed to the lieutenant his discovery. The hull was stuffed with bags of white powder. Gunpowder stores were laced through the timber spear and bow of the boat as well. Obviously, the craft had a clandestine purpose.

Takamatsu was summoned and asked to explain the seriousness of this find. In a low tone he replied, "We are an aware people. Preparedness is a virtue in our land." He went on, "It is like to your President Jefferson who said, 'Eternal vigilance is the price of freedom.'" TJ was taken aback by the breadth of Takamatsu's knowledge of American history, much less the answer itself. Nonetheless, the lieutenant ordered the grounding and inspection of all small boats, with removal of any powdery substances by the prisoners.

VI

The thing TJ was absolutely resolute in was his faith. In Sasebo, no Catholic church existed. From the beginning of his strict German American upbringing, he attended Catholic schools. He spanned years as an altar boy, singer, lectern reader, Communion minister, usher, envelope collector, and eventual parish council leader. He occasioned the daily mass when he could. His devotion to his faith was steadfast and without compromise in his beliefs. Throughout his enlistment, he carried his favorite archbishop's writings in his knapsack to read when doubts availed.

Even in this part of the world, he felt that the defeated could benefit from some "good news." Yet, in impartiality, the Japanese were called derogatory names, which he promptly denounced to his crew. Likewise, there was little tolerance for physical cruelty and abuse. Early on, he himself was teased regarding his last name, which was of Germanic heritage. The experience of xenophobia prompted him to articulate it in an English vernacular. He would make sure no room was allowed for questioning his own allegiance and loyalty in the wartime theater.

So, he set out on a personal mission. During his off-duty moments, he researched the broader area for a Catholic diocese close to his base. His efforts led him to contact a Jesuit community in Nagasaki. On a particular afternoon, he telephoned a priest there named Fr. Raphael, who listened to TJ's hopes and aspirations. The priest responded, "I have much to say on this subject, my son. However, are you ready to feel small and insignificant?" Puzzled, TJ replied, "I am open, Father." The priest offered, "If you come to Nagasaki, I will meet you."

TJ orchestrated plans with command for a weekend leave to travel. He left by train for Nagasaki, a hundred miles away. From the window, he could see the devastation wreaked on the terrain. All had collapsed to muddy dust. He stepped off at the Nagasaki stop and immediately saw a black-robed man with a Roman collar. They met and exchanged greetings. He took him to the center of the city.

"Look around Nagasaki," Fr. Raphael began, and then pointed outward. "There stands a figure. It is a young mother holding a baby, charred, disfigured, and burned to death. Next to it is a statue of St. Francis Xavier. Both, meters away from the blast. The history of our relationship with the Japanese is steeped in interrogations, brutality, and torture." He went on, "You say you wish to build a church in Sasebo?" TJ cleared his voice with a look of dismay and replied, "Well, I hope, Father. I feel we are rebuilding everything else."

They walked further until Fr. Raphael sat on a large stone. He spoke up again with a story. "There was a Christian woman in this city who, in the middle of a cold Japanese winter, was stripped bare and made to sit on a rock. By day seven, she was waist-up in snow. She survived for two weeks until she expired. I am now sitting on that same stone." He fixed TJ with a direct glance. "This very land you see, the Church paid for with countless lives. Every turn you will take stumbles into the question of peril and persecution of faith." He paused with a sigh. "Do you know the depth of what you are requesting?"

The lieutenant, feeling rather small now as Fr. Raphael had predicted, hesitated in reply. "I am not entirely sure."

The priest continued, "We tend to claim the places where our faith is tested the most. We reflect it in the world's beautiful art and dominions of worship in the most desacralized areas. It is exactly what our faith asks us to do. Our testimony has no bounds!"

"So, it has always begun in doubt and conflict?"

"Yes," said the priest, "the struggle seems to be the foundation in the resurrection of our faith. So, it is here indeed we begin."

TJ returned to Sasebo. He knew what he was asking. Building a church was no easy task. He could not labor the prisoners into the faith by submission—much less the military, as command would balk at the proposition. He hoped for a miracle. Indeed, he prayed for one.

That evening, the lieutenant reached into his shirt and felt his dog tags against his chest. Funny, he had never read them until now. Engraved was his enlistment year of 1942. He knew 1946 was his discharge year. Until now, he had always hoped his discharge would be honorable. He thought to himself, "Maybe an early furlough or granted discharge would work?" He had never felt this strong a calling before. It was a tether between two duties—one for his honor, one for his soul.

It turned November. Early morning dustings of snow were clinging to the last cherry tree blossoms. The tall cedar needles on the hillside dripped with melting ice. The locals still put bare feet to the terrain. Western shoes were freely distributed among them, but were neatly shelved with no detectable wear.

Sasebo was rebuilding more quickly now. Families scurried to winterize their homes and their sacred shrines. The locals shellacked the beams of the gates, referred to as *tori*. The gates would beacon a bright orange, even in dusk light conditions. It served a focal point for the many to pause, bow, and walk under on the way to and from daily work.

Finally, new orders came in. In the occupation phase of Sasebo, command was to move U.S. Navy ships and supplies to the new harbor front. Sasebo was beginning its transformation into a fortification base. It became a command post for watchful American troops to step-stone into Korea from the south. It was clear Japan no longer had a foothold in Korea's occupation. Another front was materializing. The Japanese papers implied the "Russian bear" was clawing into the north part of Korea. America was preparing again yet for an anticipated clash.

It alarmed the troops. Two countries' standoff, popularly dubbed "cold," was to partition Korea into two states. TJ scratched his head thinking, "It seems we're into the same land grab as brought about the European conflict."

A command dictum was released to relocate all prisoners to Nagasaki, as a labor force would be needed for an arsenal buildup in the occupied Kyushu corridor. TJ and crew were instructed to accompany their prisoners until further orders were given. Once again, President Truman and the generals were co-plotting another strategy. Most of the troops were entering their third and fourth year in the Pacific Rim. They had proved their service, loyalty, and mission worthiness to their commanders. Nonetheless, they were getting fatigued and they hoped that a break would soon come their way. The lieutenant could not help but read a dated *Guam Pacific Rim Newspaper* that made it all too clear to him. On the front page, a synopsis of the war conflicts and movements was printed in plain sight: *1945 Yalta Conference, Soviet leader Stalin incites war with Japan three months after Nazi Germany's defeat. August 9th, Soviet forces declare war on Japan. August 9th, United States forces drop the second atomic bomb on Nagasaki.*

Even though he and his division had witnessed the bomb dropping three months earlier, Nagasaki was still in shock as a chosen city. It had been one of the few places open to international trade since the 1800s. Again, Kokura had been spared by the mystical shield of clouds.

The PT-109s were crowded with prisoners on the requested

move. The lieutenant and crew were instructed to rendezvous at battleship island, Hashima, ten miles outside Nagasaki. Here they docked and waived off the prisoners to a new command. The lieutenant remembered the beautifully erected camp in Sasebo constructed in such great detail. No such establishment was apparent here. He approached and spoke to the officer in charge, particularly making note of the skills of the men he had brought. The commanding officer briefly sneered saying, "The prison laborers will be picking through their rubble here. Your command, Lieutenant, has been relieved now." They saluted in duty, and TJ and crew sped away into the bay harbor.

As the city slid more into view, the devastation was all the more evident. However, the leftover buildings still standing revealed shapes of foreign influence. TJ remarked, "We were not the first ones here. Our ancestors have ventured here before." At the shoreline, gable-roofed homes with sweeping Cape Cod porches allowed panoramic views to the open seas. Christian crosses and statuaries of saints were intermixed with reclined Buddhas. Narrow swaths of land interrupting the water allowed channels for trade. It struck TJ like a small row of warehouse structures positioned for open business. Large European scales stamped with Portuguese and Dutch emblems presented next. The scene summoned the memory of a once busy exchange of spices, tobacco, and bread for sought-after silk, fish, and crafted wood products. Synergistically, it blended local crafted artistry with European design throughout the dwellings. It was familiar to the men to see their known heritage inherent in the construction. TJ began to think that he was witnessing the best possible sign of democracy and imperialism in sync, and he tucked away this insight in the belief that he could use this mindset going forward. The fleet of 109s steered into the land-based piers and the men disembarked from their vessels.

Remnants of a bustling trade were apparent as the shops and carts faced each other to exchange goods. From a stone's throw away, the lieutenant could see a slope-roofed building with the Christian cross on top. He allowed his crew leave for the afternoon.

He went to the steps of the church, where he found a propped-up sign that stated *All are welcome*, with *Pastor Raphael* engraved underneath. He pulled open the large wooden door, which creaked to announce his entrance. He viewed an altar with a simple crucifix on top. He took five steps and genuflected, then slid into a pew and put the kneeler down. He performed the sign of the cross and started to pray. Under his breath he said an Act of Contrition, Our Father, and Hail Mary. He searched his trousers with his hand and pulled out rosary beads. He smiled at the memory of receiving these from his girl back home. He flashed back to rowing a boat on Lake Danoon, where he had serenaded and vowed his love to her.

He met Helen at the candy counter of Sears and Roebuck. He was employed as a furniture hand in lifting and moving around the parcels on the third floor. As often as he could, he would jog down the back stairwell to the first-floor candy counter for a reward. He had a weakness for sweets. It was there he met the shy but keenly witted girl. She would smile and suggest what had been made fresh that day. TJ always looked forward to her recommendations. With pretty, unassuming, and calming charm, she flirted her own brand of bobby sox and finely knitted sweaters that framed her brunette hair and delicate smile. It was just a matter of time until a suggested ice cream down at the local stand was in line for a Saturday afternoon. When he found out her name, he recalled studying the mythological story of Helen in his high school Greek and Latin classes. She was said to have been the most beautiful woman in the world. She was to be married to a king but was abducted by a prince, resulting in the Trojan War. As the story goes, she was reclaimed by her true love and brought back to her home Sparta. TJ knew and could recount the legend well.

In an attempt to stay on task, he grasped the rosary tighter and prayed the ten Hail Marys and Lord's Prayer in sequence.

His mind drifted between Helen and the Virgin Mary. After all, her full name was Helen Mary. It had been a long while since he had been in church. The chaplain's quarters on the cruiser ships were not the same. He looked up and saw the statue of the Virgin on a side corner. He felt the struggle within himself. He knew he was embarking on a new journey if allowed early discharge. The ensuing months in this foreign land would be difficult. He felt the divinely inspired work of bringing the church to Sasebo was hinting a task too great to comprehend. His eyes captured the compassionate, open arms of the statue of Mary; her tender smile seemed to answer the needs of generations looking upon her. His mind flashed back to the blue eyes of Helen waiting in Milwaukee. He wondered how these constraining visions which were summoning him could meet any resolution. He stood up from the pew and walked over to the statue. Gazing into the face of Mary, he began to see the face of Helen transfixed. He knelt down and attempted to further rationalize his words: "What is the difference between the face that launched a thousand ships and the face that brought the new light of life into the world?" As he bowed his head in silence, he suddenly felt a hand on the shoulder. He looked up to see Fr. Raphael as he said, "I'm glad you came." The intensity of the moment brought up tears in the lieutenant's eyes from the years of sleepless tossing. He stood and turned to him as if directionless. The priest exuded a compassionate embrace. He uttered, "All will be well."

Fr. Raphael invited him through a hall behind the sacristy into an outdoor porch area. A great view of the harbor bay area was seen, scattered with ships. A U.S. battleship flew the American flag like a proud peacock showing its feathers. There were two chairs overlooking the scene. The priest asked, "You are Catholic?"

TJ responded, "I am."

"Would you like some water or tea?"

"Is it iced tea?"

The priest gently rotated his head to the right and then left. "You won't find America's cold drinks or barrack mess halls here. You drink the local tea. It is matcha. It is called the 'tea of life' here. When you drink matcha, you ingest the entire leaf and receive one hundred percent of its nutrients." He continued, "It is like those who live the faith here. It is a reminder that to walk as a Catholic is to walk one hundred percent in the nourishment of faith. So you are asked to walk the faith, keep the faith, and endure all things, in all trials and in all times."

TJ nodded and politely took the tea to sip. Instantly he sputtered out a cough—he was not accustomed to the flavor or potency. He gestured with his hand and said, "I think I'll have water."

The priest chuckled. "Let us walk the grounds and I will show you what it is like here."

Fr. Raphael pointed out the back hills of the mountainous terrain, where the land was manicured cleanly to accommodate the footings of the church structure. He explained that the raptor crossbeams boasted timbers of twenty inch-diameter pine. The logs were sawed by hand in the higher mountainous areas and dragged by horses to the mills to be stripped and carved. The women would hand-sew horsehair strips and wrap them around the beams to anchor bamboo pole reinforcement. It would take days for each sixteen-foot beam to arrive, especially in winter. The local woodsmen were skilled in shaping the finials into wings for the temples and shrines. They would use these skills to interlock the beams for supporting the walls and notching them to receive the thatch for the roof.

He wandered to a statue. "Have you seen the patron saint Francis Xavier?" The priest explained, "They carve these figures from choice cedar pieces. They are given pictures of saints and mimic the eyes with pearl shells and faces with abalone and onyx. Notching wood posteriorly creates the opening to the face from behind, so no imperfections from chiseling are seen by the viewer. Hair is then placed on and dyed black to cover any imperfections.

They are masters at woodworking and smoothing surfaces with shellac so that lines are not detected." He went on, "These skills and techniques have been passed on through generations. For the past two thousand years, the influence of Buddhism from India and China brought these trades. However, it was in the tradition of their Shinto religion that integrated the suffering of Siddhartha into the worship of their ancestors and nature spirits. They called it sacred power, better known as syncretism. That has changed now. Their connection between today and ancient past has exploded in a world they no longer trust nor understand. That is what I have witnessed in the coming of Catholicism here. In time you will see too."

They took a stroll past the fish stalls. TJ had not yet tasted the local food. He glanced at the priest, wondering whether it was safe to eat. Fr. Raphael returned the look with a large grin. He stated, "It is all I eat, and I am still here." The array was enormous. Octopus, scallops, squid, crab, sea bass, snapper, and blue fin tuna gleamed with rich color and freshness. They ordered lunch. The fish was sliced into thin bite-sized pieces with scales and skin trimmed and pulled away. The rice was sticky and clumped in a way that TJ had never tasted in America. A green leaf substance was mashed at his table and placed next to a fermented bed of ginger. He learned the fresh green pasty substance was wasabi. He was forewarned it was sharp to taste. The priest caught TJ's disinterest and asked him, "Do you like American mustard and horseradish?" He replied, "I have it all the time with my bratwurst back home." Fr. Raphael stated he would eat it whole if TJ did not at least try a taste, so the lieutenant dipped his chopstick into the substance for a morsel of flavor. To his surprise, it was earthy and strong but without heat. "Not bad," he delighted in saying. He gestured to the fisherman's wife serving and requested more. She delivered with the typical *"Hai"* in Japanese, and afterward she and her husband brought two small ceramic cups to the table. The hosts proceeded to pour a clear-looking wine for their patrons.

TJ was curious about the crystal-clear liquid. He decided that he would only take a sip—since he had had a previous experience that left him unstable on his feet. The priest took both cups and performed a blessing and short prayer before handing one of them to TJ. He raised his cup and ceremonially waited for TJ to raise his. Then Fr. Raphael sounded for all to hear, "To the repatriation of faith!" The two men clicked the fine ceramic cups together and deftly downed them.

The priest concluded the meal with, "I will give you a history lesson and then show you how to build the church."

They proceeded into the courtyard and paused once more at the statue of Francis Xavier. Fr. Raphael then pronounced, "We are where it began for the Catholic Church and the martyrdom that followed its reception in this country." They strolled the grounds and TJ counted twenty-six sculpted figures standing like gate-keepers around the church. Names and epitaphs were inscribed on them. The priest started, "Initially, the Japanese thought these foreigners were from India and that this Christianity was to be likened to the new Buddhism." He proceeded, gesturing around, "You have counted the martyrs who suffered persecution, torture, and death under the Japanese since the mid-sixteenth century. Look at the sculptures closely and you can see the thorns, burns, nails, and brutality that pierced their bodies. They walked to bring Jesus and the mission of Christ here." The priest turned to go on. "Now, look over here and see the parched figures sil-houetted in the stone. Many, as I said, have walked the faith and never let go until their last breath, then and till today. This has been demanded from both non-Japanese and Japanese to the wit-ness of Christ. Some left, and rightly so. But these figures saw the universality of the mission to spread the Word against all odds. Rest assured, even now, they express resistance to the way. The Japanese are steeped in their long history of ancestors, deities, and beliefs in all that is living and not. They see it not as an idolatry or paganism practice, but as all things having a sacred power and energy. It is the deed that goes awry, not the person." He paused to take a breath. "Ironically, it is not far from the written Gospels. It seems we suffer from the same but have different awareness, and thus realizations." He paused and continued, "Both require much of the human spirit and grant an experience of mindfulness and healing. Both have suffered the extreme in the brutality of human hands and mass destructive weapons. We obligate ourselves to pray and meditate on the mystery of both."

After the priest finished, TJ asked, "So, how many here are with the faith?"

The priest's shoulders stooped with a sigh. "We are less than one percent as a religion here." He hesitated but went on, "Yet, we represent one hundred percent of the tests of faith." He suddenly stopped to look at his watch. "Now, I must excuse myself and prepare for Mass."

Fr. Raphael walked toward the church. Before entering, he signaled to the lieutenant to attend the service. The pews filled up with less than fifty people, though built for at least five hundred. The attendees sat up at the front. The mass was said in Japanese. Even the homily was in Japanese. During consecration they got on their knees. At Communion TJ saw that all the locals came up to receive, many of them disfigured and hobbling. He was transfixed by this evidence of the ills of the war. The burn wounds and bandage wrappings around faces, limbs, and feet were prevalent. The people shuffled up slowly, seemingly to overcome the grief of pain. It was if they were lining up for the salvation of the sacrament. In the end, a final blessing was given. Yet at the conclusion, no one rose to leave.

Suddenly, Fr. Raphael announced to the nuns in the rear pews that it was time. Until then TJ had not noticed them sitting quietly with basins of water and white strips of cloth. Naturally, he was curious to see what was to happen next. He was used to having coffee and donuts after Mass in the States. However, there was no such reception here. The nuns filed into the front pews and placed the cloths and the basins of water in their laps. One person at a time, they removed worn and soiled cloth around skin areas that were blemished or rotting. They rinsed the new cloths in water and wrapped them gently around the peeling, slow to heal tissue.

TJ sat and placed his hand on his chin, silently observing. He thought of offering a hand to help, but somehow he was struck incapacitated in the same way the bombed victims were. It was something he wished he had never seen. It was something too painful to talk about ever after in his life. It would become something he would forever see in the crucifix above an altar.

The next morning, he compelled himself into his regimented run through the streets of Nagasaki. He realized it was his first jog without the command of his crew. He felt the juxtaposition of the energy and strength of his legs against the locals' steady toil of picking up rubble, sweeping the streets, and preparing new pathways. He slowed after a three-mile circle.

It was then he noticed a woman with an unusual broom—the straw head looked tied in a fan-like style at various angles, and it captured debris cleanly in one swoop. She looked up at him as if to let him pass, but he reached into his pocket and pulled out a pack of gum. He removed one, put it in his mouth, and chewed purposefully as if instructing a technique. He walked over and attempted to hand her a piece. She bowed instantly as if in gratitude. However, she did not take it. He offered it again and she still did not take it. Finally, he reached his hand forward and grabbed her wrist gently, and he turned her hand over to place the piece of gum in her palm. She bowed again and turned to continue her sweeping. As he walked away he could see two young boys without shoes playing curbside in the street with a stick. He continued to walk, then half glanced back in curiosity. He noticed that the woman took the gum piece from her palm, tore it in half, and gave it to the boys. He hesitated for a moment and then walked on. Being close to the steps of the church once more, he stepped up and turned slightly to cast his eyes back. He saw the women and two boys bow in unison to him. He nodded his head forward and continued into the church.

To his surprise, Fr. Raphael was up reading a wrinkled newspaper. The lieutenant could smell coffee brewing. "Hot joy!" he exclaimed, "May I have a cup?" The priest remarked, "No matcha? It tastes better after a run." TJ replied, "Not for me!"

The older man retrieved a tall ceramic cup from a cabinet and poured a morning joe for his guest, who then relaxed into a chair, uninterested in anything else. He was offered a platter of soft, green, oval-shaped, sponge-like cakes. He assumed that it was some type of donut. He also knew that the pervasive green color meant he would get his matcha anyhow. He obliged to take one and put it to the rigors of his lips and jaw. To his surprise, it collapsed quickly in his mouth and tasted more like a dry cottage cheese. He exclaimed to the priest, "What is this?"

The priest turned to the next page in his paper without skipping a beat. "It's bean curd. Do you like?"

"Not bad."

"It is the nectar treat for the local gastronomy. It is not a matter of whether you like it or not. It is their breakfast, unless you prefer rice."

TJ acted pleased and resumed eating. "Anything new in the paper today?"

The priest replied, "Not sure, this paper is dated the second of August." He followed, "It is nice to know Nagasaki is cloudy today with afternoon showers. We now prefer it that way. Besides, it is good for the rice fields and lotus plants."

Looking out to the unusually clear skies, TJ cajoled the priest, "If I may, this would be an opportune day for instructions in church construction."

Fr. Raphael followed, "Oh, yes, I forgot to tell you." He continued, "I have it all taken care of. You will see it is best to let the locals do the work. They have the plans for the church. They will construct accordingly. All that is needed is the plot, and they will make it fit." He further questioned, "That is something you have?"

TJ hesitated. "Well, I do have an idea. But I will need to get clearance from the base for the area."

The priests, somewhat surprised, blurted, "I thought you were in command there?"

"Well, I guess I am. I am not sure who to check with, though."

The priest contested, "You have answered your own question." He insisted, "Don't hesitate, Lieutenant, the time is now!"

TJ asked, "How will I get the laborers?"

"The place you jog around in the mornings. This is the place where the skilled men, women, and children will come from to build the church. It is your job to make sure they can utilize the empty prison base. They will be comfortable there. I am sure any superior commander will be pleased. They will compliment you for such great use of the materials, ingenuity, and spiritual uplift in transforming the camp." Fr. Raphael then stood and said resolutely, "Time to start!"

Thus, TJ began to gather up workers, who gathered up what little they possessed. He called back to his crew, and boats were summoned. A total of forty-five were at hand to build the first church in Sasebo. Fr. Raphael gave them a blessing as they boarded the torpedo crafts. The lieutenant boarded the last boat and requested that the good Father come along. He returned, "I'll make the visit before you know it!" "Not too soon," TJ quipped. "I'd like to have the front door standing!" The lieutenant unsecured the lines, saluted, and waved off. The priest returned the gesture with a sign of the cross and bowed.

They arrived at sunset in Sasebo. The crew jumped off the boat and secured the lines. The workers paused long before disembarking, standing on the boat with eyes closed and faced to the sun.

TJ was pleased to see Huggins and Yaz and even warmed to Takamatsu. The laborers were to proceed in an orderly way, unpack their sacks, and settle into their new living quarters. Somewhat impatiently, TJ waited and watched them stand motionlessly against the low sun. He asked, "What are they waiting for?" Takamatsu stepped forward to speak. "If I may, sir, they have left the place they have known. It was a place they believed they were born into and would die into." Takamatsu continued, "Like the sun once high in the sky, something exploded between their lives. The sun is now shadowed between the morning sunrise and the evening sunset. This is the constant they remember in the morning and in the evening. They are unsure what is in between." TJ returned, "We are building their future now, in between." Takamatsu bowed politely in a ceremonial way.

The base seemed much more active with the hammering of construction noise for the new American naval site and academy. As TJ walked up the slope, another officer met him. "Lieutenant," his lips spouted, "I am Captain Henderson. I have been awaiting your return. I have orders to assume command of your men. You have been approved to continue your operation for the church construction on the prison grounds. You can retain a few crewmen to instruct and oversee the premises with the laborers brought." TJ was delighted but curious to follow up and question. "Who gave the approval so quickly, let alone knew of such plans?" "Why, Colonel R. Berringer, sir, First Division squad commander at Okinawa." "Hmm," TJ pondered for a moment. He did not recall a Commander Berringer of such ranking at Okinawa. It was well known the First Division struck ahead before he had arrived with the second for the cleanup. The lieutenant pressed on, "Captain, would you happen to know his first name?" The other replied, "I believe Raphael, sir."

It did not take long for TJ to assemble his oversee crew and workers brought from Nagasaki. Takamatsu was instructed to address them in the local ways and language. He assisted in determining the abilities of each of the workers, then selected and grouped the men and women that possessed parallel skills in carpentry, weaving, and construction.

TJ spoke and his words were reiterated through Takamatsu's interpretation: "You have been brought here to build a church. It will be a Catholic church, much like the one built in the Nagasaki. You will be allowed to speak your language and observe certain practical traditions. In addition, English will be taught and spoken, especially to the children. You will have food, clothing, and shelter for your basic needs." He continued, "We will honor the sacrifices of the men and women who came here not only to repatriate, but to spread the new democracy and faith. You will each be given a Bible to assure your efforts." He paused to scan attentiveness around and then resumed. "You have been given the construction plans previously. We will start tomorrow and will be steadfast in these efforts until the final crucifix is placed on top of the cupola. You are now dismissed." The lieutenant retreated to his barracks. He was spent after all he had seen and experienced in Nagasaki. He took a deep breath and lay back on his familiar cot. He drifted off in sleep into the dreams of his youth.

VII

It was an informative time at St. Sebastian's School. The annual project was commissioned through the monsignor of the parish. The fundraiser put forth was to construct a small chapel in honor of the anniversary of St. Sebastian. It was a daunting adventure and a laborious task. TJ's eighth grade education was coming to an end. Yet, in looking back, he realized it marked the beginning of his self-aware intent to give back for his formative years at school and church.

He saw the project as a test for him. After all, in his youthful work experience, physical labor only exerted itself in the delivery of neighborhood newspapers and the occasional lawn mow job. What haunted him was the stark image of St. Sebastian. He walked past the statue daily. He squinted at the morbidly inflicted arrow wounds all over his body. By some less dramatic means, he believed he, too, would be inflicted by not adhering to the strict Catholic doctrine and creed of faith.

What served him most in this venture were his attributes of work ethic and ability to unify classmates' passions through team building. He inspired with example through his natural aptitudes. His artistic designs inspired the developing trade talents in each of his classmates. It soon became a mission for them to unify their gifts to build different parts of the building. A nearby collapsed stone creek with concrete mix laid the foundations. A worn basketball court was re-sanded for flooring. As the block work and stucco with paint was finishing drying, a constructed eight-foot roof with tide trusses was lifted up to secure the walls. In the end, because of his exemplary teamwork and direction, TJ was selected to place the gilded cross on top of the cupola. He steadied himself at the top of the tall leaning ladder and positioned the large crucifix upon the gable on high. He deftly took out the mallet from his belt and nails from his shirt pocket and began hammering the cross into place. He remembered reaching across the base to place one last secure nail. Just then, he felt his weight slip away from his feet, his balance teetering. The ladder slid away. Aghast, he dangled, instinctively reaching for the base of the cross to grasp on to. He hollered for help while suspended in the air. His classmates, once stepped back to observe the dignified edifice, darted now to his aid. They lifted the ladder from its angled plop on the ground and repositioned it under his feet. TJ had never experienced his socket joints stretched to dislocation in an attempt to resist gravity's pull back to Earth. Once he recovered his breath, he stepped back down slowly, backed away, and looked up at his defying work on top of the chapel.

He could see and understand his fears. As he observed he had not been alone in hanging, he began to understand something more. The sculpted figure of Christ on the crucifix reflected that strained reach. The final placed cross was secure and defined the work that was now finished. It had a scary end but brought a new awareness that would last him till the present. His conviction to unquestioning faith defined him against a state of letting go and not knowing. That was the test then. It would be retried again later.

He awoke in early morning to the chattering of the workers' hammers. The women and children were busy gathering up thatch and sweeping the premises. It was one of many clear days as the laborers filled and clamored about the whole perimeter of the building site. Cedar timbers and bamboo arrived and were inspected by the craftsmen. Immediately, at each end, a chisel notching technique was implemented to cradle additional notched timber, thus creating neat stacks.

The lieutenant walked about to observe. He could see no signs of measurement tools. Undoubtedly, the craftsmen's senses of sight and touch were fully utilized. TJ called the interpreter over and questioned, "Where did they learn to be so precise without instruments?" Takamatsu answered, "If I may, it is a relationship between the forest and man that has been here for thousands of years. It has been taught through our ancestors in the sacred living trees of the forest." Flummoxed, TJ simply looked at Takamatsu who beckoned and offered, "May I go on, sir?" The lieutenant nodded his head. "Our ancestors are in those trees. We surrender the trees as we honor the ancestors that gave us these gifts. We are to be mindful of them, respectful of them, precise with our efforts, and to express gratitude to them. For we will join them someday in this connection." TJ waved his hand to stop him and said, "I've had enough of this talk." He paused. "Let's get this straight. We are building a Catholic church. Enough of this gibberish—the next thing you will say is that the ancestors will come down as animals and bow to the workers."

The Americans observed a strange custom which all Japanese family members would do. At night, the women and children would gather flowers and twigs of various shapes on the grounds. Since bamboo was in abundance in this part of the island, they would break off a stem, whittle it down, and smooth the edges. They would notch the bottom and fit it tightly onto a piece of cedar. The workers would then transplant them into the huts. On a particular occasion, Private Huggins was ordered to perform an impromptu inspection of the living quarters. He noticed within each dwelling the twigs, branches, and delicate flowers which had been gathered outside. They had been arranged, twisted, and banded together to shape a whole—simple yet graceful and eye-catching arrangements in bamboo containers had been created. Instead of standing on the tables, they were placed into wood scrap block shelves on the walls at about eye level. It was almost as if they were venerating something, yet nothing significant to the private was to be seen. The technique was very three dimensional, as it could be turned in a variety of heights and positions to create an aesthetic, almost like conveying a strong sense of space identity. The children would sometimes take them and leave them at the quarter ends of the camp cabins under eaves to collect rainwater.

One day, Huggins stopped a young boy on this repeated journey back and forth. The private asked, "*Otokonoko (boy in Japanese)!* What is in your hand?" The boy did not know how to respond. The private then said," Do you speak some English?" The boy gestured with his fingers. He gestured a small space between his thumb and index finger. Huggins took that to mean a little. The private then spoke in broken Japanese, "*Nan? Nan?*" The boy spoke, "*Ikebana,*" and ran back to his quarters.

When the private returned to his barrack, he looked for Takamatsu. He ran into Yaz and asked if he knew what *ikebana* meant. The code talker looked puzzled. He spoke, "In Navajo it means 'bring life to flowers.'"

Huggins responded, "That is strange, since the flowers were cut and seemingly dying."

Walking by, Takamatsu overheard what they were saying. He took the liberty to remark. "If I may, the flowers are brought from the earth and are given new existence through the delicate arrangement in a vessel. It is to show life to us. They symbolize harmony among heaven, man, and Earth." He paused briefly. "It is for the human to bind nature and creation into this technique. Note the three in the use of one line, one flower, and one piece of foliage to demonstrate the nature of shape, texture, and color. That is all that is needed to be one."

The private scorned, "So, it's one of those voodoo-type practices again." Takamatsu bowed and walked to the door to exit. Huggins turned to Yaz and said, "These people sure have some strange customs."

Yaz smiled and said nothing. The private walked to the door but turned back to Yaz before leaving. "How did you know what that *ikebana* meant? Is that something you learned in your culture as an Indian?"

Yaz smiled and politely responded, "I can see why you might think so. I guess it is kind of a cultural thing."

The workers were making good time with the foundation and structural walls of the church. The young boys were smoothing the interfaces between the fittings and interlocking joints for a seamless blend. Sometimes they would work on a single surface all day. It was if the individual component was more important than the construct of the building. The crew found it interesting to watch. They would even observe replacement of the timbers that did not have the right color, camber, or grain to match the subsequent timber used. Everything had a specific place, allowing precision and order for the building to proceed in shape. As the sidewalls took definition, you began to see the lifting and arch towards the ceiling. Comfits were shaped to complement the eaves and create open-air soffits for circulation. The four center support pillars within the church stood to the rooflines connected by a floating wooden rafter, which was held by metal chain linked around it as if to stabilize direction and defy any displacing movement.

Such vertical supports mimicked those of the buildings that had survived the atomic blast. The constructs floated within a sleeve of structural support so that they could withstand the tremble of earthquakes. They termed this "positive camber." In doing so, freedom to express a sweeping roof could delicately balance the transcending aesthetics, natural beauty, and tranquility. Ingeniously, the depth of the overhanging eaves controlled the amount of daily arching sunlight and self-regulated the temperatures throughout the interior. Partitions were placed within frames to offer sliding in-wall screen paper doorways to further adjust seasonal temperatures. It was apparent that the local laborers knew and applied their inherited skills in harmony with nature.

Huggins shrugged and commented to Yaz, "I hope they don't turn out to make automobiles like they do these structures."

The next day, TJ woke early before sunrise broke. He took his shower turned up to tepid temperature, which was the highest he was accustomed to. He noticed the plumbing was astutely hidden behind a veneer of overlapping *tatami*. He placed his hand against the tatami to sense its support and thickness. He could feel the thin consistency of its skin-like sheets, taken from the trees his laborers were working with. The paper smell it emanated when dampened from the shower scented the room like cedar locked in a closet. The Japanese industry of harvesting and utilizing the natural elements consistently breathed into their construction of things. Even the multiple-level water valves easily operated with a pull of a bamboo handle. A connected loop of braided string hung conveniently for when soap invaded one's eyes.

He rinsed and looked out a high chin-level window. Through the dense trees surrounding his barrack he could barely see the silhouettes that began to appear. Men workers began to gather around a circular makeshift water trench. He could see early morning fog-like steam rise from the water's surface. One by one, they rolled up their worn khaki trousers to just above the knees and gradually waded into the water to the calf. They circled around the container, hovering like mourning doves until coming to rest on the edge of a section of cedar rounds. As they sat with feet immersed in the water, they would exhale a soothed bellow of "ahh." They would remain for no longer than ten minutes before the next entourage would sequence through. Each would express the same relief.

The lieutenant readied himself. After the morning briefing for the day's schedule, he addressed Takamatsu. "What is this pond of water for the laborers to soak their feet in?" Takamatsu explained, "It is called the *onsen*. The water in the Earth is brought up to surface and used by the men to soak and relieve the aches in the feet. It has natural radon gas and bubbles throughout the water to relieve soreness. It helps them work on their feet for long hours and be productive without prodding or complaint." The lieutenant listened astutely and replied, "Good. I am glad they have the means to do so."

Later, he walked over to the pond area for a closer look. He could view clear through the water to the rocky layer on the bottom. The rocks seemed volcanic and treacherous to step on. He could smell no odor. The sight invited him to partake in the bubbles and steam concoction. He decided to take off his shoes and socks for a go and ended up staying in it much longer than the ten minutes he had timed for the others.

As he returned to his quarters he could hear the sound of squirreling feet and child-like giggles echo between quarters. At the foot of his door, he noticed a small colored paper-like figure with folded angles. He bent down to pick it up with the intent of tidying up. However, he noted that it appeared deliberate in its shape. As he inspected it on eye level, he noticed the details of the folds shaped a bird-like form and realized the creation of a swan. He thought to himself, "Is there a message inside?" As he unfolded the paper he could see the intricate lines unveiled a detailed map of a folding technique. He had hoped for a secret code.

Walking to his desk, he sat down and began to lay the paper out on the flat surface of the credenza. He unfolded the final fold delicately, as if executing a fine surgical procedure. He now had it totally exposed for any hidden cipher. Nothing. He flipped it over and over and could not see anything of usefulness. "Is this some kind of game?" he thought. He sat back for a moment and then thought to toss it into the trash. The he looked at it again and started to follow the lines back and reconstruct the figure crease by crease to the way he had found it. It soon became a challenge to recreate the formless sheet back to its original intent. As he worked it, it began to reshape into the wings and downward beak of the bird he had picked up. Finally it was complete again. "Yes," he exclaimed. "I did it!" He held it up to the light and pondered the uncommon artifact. At first, he had thought it a swan; now, he saw it truly as a crane.

Throughout the ensuing weeks, his routine walking inspections included glancing through the windows. Interestingly, for the workers and their families, the lieutenant could not spot any bags of household trash, unlike was habit to his command and crew. His checkups included listening in on the English lessons taught to the children. After their dismissal, he pondered about the time used in the extra activities of each day. Every time he came into view, the children kept a shy distance, scattering from him. Throughout the grounds, he could not see any discard or hint of disposal bins lying about. Even when a box was seen, often nothing was to be found in it. At the very least, he looked for the paper used in school for learning. He pondered whether it was being further displayed as art folded in decorative shapes and figures.

The details of the church began shape. Slabs of milled old-growth pines were swept into the four corners and erected to give height. The workers honed and chiseled joint surfaces for the square angles to notch neatly and slide tightly into place with a tap of the mallet.

The sight of this progress pleased TJ as he strolled through the building, looking every direction. At the lieutenant's side, Private Huggins reached for a dormant mallet on the workers' floor. He questioned its usefulness without metal parts. He could see the intricate twine that encapsulated the handle of bamboo, wrapped in a serpentine fashion around the end. It reminded him of the handle of the kanto, a Japanese officer's sword, that he had picked up in the fighting on Okinawa. In a sudden manner he turned to face and rest his forehead into a newly constructed corner. He pressed into it harder and lifted a forearm to cover his eyes as if suffering under a burden. With face concealed, he began to stutter with multiple coughs that morphed unaware into a wailing weep.

VIII

Huggins' state of traumatic daze took him back to that past time. The memory was still quite vivid to him and in that moment snuck up on him like a nightmare in wakefulness. "Why, why?!" he kept repeating.

He remembered taking the hill after a month's slog on Okinawa. Even his commander left his compassion in the foot-hills, summoning a deeply festered anger beyond what was ever felt before. The imperialists kept retreating and never hinted at surrender. The smoking machine guns lay empty in the low grasses of the hills as the Americans climbed up to the island plateau. Huggins cursed, tripping over one fallen after another as he focused ahead in the climb. He recalled falling once to a knee over the carcass of a pint-sized defender trapped behind his weapon. "Animals," he would describe them who had un-expectedly mowed down his comrades just an hour before. The occasional fire would be heard at a distance. It did not deter their march to achieve the strategic survey which the upper plateau of the isle afforded. The orientation of the enemy was unclear since

the scarce clearings would not give away position. As they surrounded the cave mounds of earth on top of the mesa, they were
struck by the stillness in the air.

The commander motioned with a finger to the men gathered.
His expression was of sullen concern. Huggins and comrades
gathered closer. The commander spoke softly, "They are in there.
They have nowhere to go. If we go in, they will certainly ambush
us." He grimly continued, "They have retreated not to surrender,
but to fight again. We can wait. Yet, if we do, they may or may
not come out." He then sighed. "We need to finish this mission
and move on. I will speaker them to exit with only the white flag
of surrender. If they do not, we will end this."

They spent the next minutes waiting. Thank goodness for
freshly packaged cigarettes to calm the nerves. In the intense island sun, Huggins took his helmet off to release the sweat from
his brow and temporarily close his eyes to bask in the rays. The
impression felt like a final benediction. A benediction of the crimson Nippon sun before the blood spilled out of it.

The order came. "Men! Start with the grenades." Instead of
being lobbed, they were thrown like a pitcher's fastball into the
depth of a catcher's glove. The explosions shook the ground as
if right under their feet. No words spoken. No sounds. No exit.
The wait and quiet seemed longer now. Huggins never prayed for
what was ahead.

He was the only one trained in the use of the equipment
he carried. He had been educated in the Department of
Forestry at Northern Arizona University in a bucolic place
called Flagstaff, Arizona. He was going to be a forester when
called up. Fire management was his training. He first learned
of managed use of fire through the Grecian method for land
preparation per agricultural seasons, with the purpose of increasing return on their fruit and olive harvests. In the forest,
fire line suppression served as a defense barrier from the living.
He became a hometown hero when wild flames were bravely

contained before encroaching on the populace in the city. At best, he considered himself the last defender of humankind against nature's uncontrolled beast.

Suddenly he heard the order from his commander: "Huggins, deploy the thrower." He checked his gauge and removed the cap to check that it was full. He could smell kerosene. In the forest, propane was used. It was considered safer, as it would die out faster and was easier to put out. He reached for his hand protectors and carefully put them on as if he was attending a proper glove affair.

As he stepped to the mouth of the cave, he paused for a moment to press the weapon on his hip for back throw and stability. He intensely looked at the ranking officer for his order. He could only wish to forget where he was and only remember his duty to country. The commander dropped his arm. Huggins let go a fiery blast into the cave. The smoke stacked and bellowed into the refuge of the sky.

It was then he woke to his hell of destruction. The Japanese surfaced in a disarray of fire. It only worsened as the din rose into the open sky from the cave. Weapons of no use sealed to their skin. Bodies put even more fiercely ablaze in the oxygenated air once outside. The cries and falling flesh in front of Huggins' eyes was a shock beyond shock. Men fell sizzling beyond pain at his feet. A dozen dropped to the ground in the slow ensuing inferno with wafts of burning flesh and bone pushing through the living. The smell alone drove all the Americans back in nasal and gastronomical uproar. After the smoke cleared and temperatures returned to a walkable ground, the Americans resumed to the next.

Huggins remembered reaching down to the parched ground to take up a glistening tempered kanto sword. His effort broke off the chalked hand still gripped around the handle. As the flesh pieces fell away, he held the tightly woven handle with sparkling jewels of pearl, abalone, and onyx stone, amazing to behold. He lifted up the meter-length blade and the reflection of the sun off of it briefly blinded him. Huggins attached it to his belt loop. It swung free from the suit of a victor. In unbeknownst trauma, he looked out to the Pacific east toward America, unaware that the day was June 24, his birthday.

IX

The laborers started to work now with few breaks. The days were getting shorter with increasing density of cool fog in the mornings. Snow hastened its entrance. The gables and ties for the roof were now being constructed. The timbers and braces of wood were all bound by straw rope. The women appeared earlier to work than the men. They would tightly weave in spiraling fashion the straw pieces of long-stem cut bamboo and then draw the straw within the camber to keep the rope from sliding off. Two on each end would tie the rope around their waists. In synchrony, they would lean back to remove the slack, and thus it would tighten similarly to a Chinese finger trap. The taut lengths were sectioned and assembled to the next timbers by the men. It became a sequenced production line of unspoken efficiency.

The laborers centered the horizontal beams for support. A bamboo strip around the log's wooden pins held the crisscross beams in place. In the past week, the phoenix structure had become more visible to the town locals. The Sasebo women and children had gathered additional thatched material in the wooded part of the forest. They had carted heaps of pressed leaves in a wooden wagon and arranged them in piles by similar sizes off the entrance to the camp. Horizontal poles were angled to the top now to hold the awaiting thatch while the ropes were secured to demarcate its position.

Takamatsu was instructed to tell the laborers to keep the roof at a steep angle. But the laborers did not understand the construction pitch was purposed to accommodate the increased air draft up. Takamatsu addressed the lieutenant on their behalf. "Sir, it is traditional with these materials for air draft and heat retention to sweep these angles less." The lieutenant considered for a moment. He remembered his grade school parish cathedral with the reliquary and bell tower. He thought of the stone construction and thought no different for this construction. The lieutenant responded, "We need the angles the way they are to accept the weight of the cupola, bell, and crucifix for all to see on top. We will proceed as said."

Takamatsu relayed the orders to the laborers. Accordingly they notched the timber angles to sixty degrees for the increased loads. The laborers shook their heads, concerned. The general drafting of heated air could lead to trouble. The thatch gathered was a type of pampas grass that could be intertwined to one meter thick as a bed of insulation. In time, it would sandwich to half that thickness due to the drying from inside and moisture retention from the foggy sea air above. The assembly was strategic and methodical from floor to roof. Men positioned protruding wooden pins along the beams to interlock the thatch in a crisscross pattern. The center point was left open for the bell and the cupola above. The gong-type bell which soon arrived was inscribed with dragons all around. Upon inspection, the lieutenant did not approve of the dragon motif; however, he changed his mind since it would be placed within a box on high, as he had few other options.

The cupola box was constructed around the bell with a cedar top base to secure the cross. The men sized the cross to measure one meter in width by two meters in height, to match the symmetry of the boxed gong bell. They crossed and notched two pieces of cypress to display the stealth and grain of the relic. Knowing the cross could not be brought in, the lieutenant had it handmade, which he expected was fully within the skills of the workers. The lieutenant provided them with a visual from a cross hanging on a chain around his neck. The Japanese artisans inspected it for a moment and proceeded. The detail and grandeur of the whittled cedar cruciform was second to none, appearing as though casted from TJ's neckpiece itself. The workers secured the base with wooden pins and dowels with tie-downs over the cupola to deter sway. A twisted cord was dropped through the roof opening and wrapped around a beam, and then the weighty showpiece was lifted by straps to the roof. Nimbly, the center beam timber was slid into the open slot for acceptance. A long cord dropped to the floor and was tied off to a side pillar. Only then was the roof secured to the base of the cupola vault. There it rested in readiness for its summoning.

The focus then turned to the inside of the church. A hearth for heating was imbedded into the floor. As was its purpose in many homes, this feature was designed to warm the space, burn incense, and even enable food preparation. No pews or chairs were planned since the Japanese were accustomed to standing, sitting, and kneeling on floors. However, tatami mats were interlocked over the entire floor for cushioning and ease of cleaning. At this point, all shoes were removed for the last touches to the interior.

Finally, the altar was addressed. Cypress was used. The planks were honed at a slight lift to accept the relics and other items on the surface. The legs were carved and bound into vertical struts as if they represented flutes of a basilica organ ready to spew forth hymns. Eight laborers gently lifted the masterpiece cypress block and carried it to the front center of the building. The lieutenant was called in to approve its placement. Upon entering the church, he gazed from front to each side and breathed a sigh of anticipated relief. "Hai," he responded in a comforting voice. The workers bowed.

The front door was all that was left to be finished. The lieutenant addressed the interpreter: "Make sure it is a split door and hinged to open wide from the center." He paused before continuing his thought—"It must be welcoming to all." He walked out the empty threshold through the sunlit beams behind him. The darkened shadows of the building came to an end as he exited, and the rays of sunlight began to outline the shape of the mounted cross on the terrain's surface before his feet. TJ turned about and faced up to the sight. He instinctively knelt for the first time in Japan.

Huggins was sent to prepare Fr. Raphael, bearing a message regarding the dedication and invocation of the future church. Meanwhile, all that remained to be completed was the entrance opening. A saved section of prime cypress timber leaned to the side. It was measured, cut, and readied for an opening, and transformed into a heavy split door, it was aligned and hung. The front face of each door had eye-level pearl inlays. They were gently pressed into eloquent crosses inside the deeply chiseled wood grain. The doors swung open effortlessly with a finger pull.

The lieutenant ordered the dismantling of the vestiges of fencing around the prison yard. The once occupied encampment was once again open to the beach break of the sea. Many of the locals previously peering from afar through the prison yard fencing could now enter. A number still remained at a distance as if the fence remained an indelible part of their lives. Only gradually did they step up to observe the newly crowned chapel. The children approached the doors to trace their fingers over the pearl cross figure. They felt its shape as if to sense the energy of this holy place.

Fr. Raphael arrived harborside to be greeted by the lieutenant. "So it is done," said the priest in greeting. "I could see the steeple float above the tree line from afar as we meandered through the bay." He continued, "Where did you come up with the details and refinements?" With slight hesitation the lieutenant replied, "Well, Father, as you know, we had a pack of good shepherds."

The priest walked through the town. Immediately, the children seemed to recognize him and ran up to him. All bowed. They proceeded to search through his pockets, hang on his long cassock, and twirl the beads hanging at his waist.

He turned a corner and shielded his eyes as the sun crested behind his destination. He squinted with delight as if beholding an inspired composition. TJ said to him, "I believe we are ready for invocation." Fr. Raphael exclaimed, "Well done!" and continued, "Let us hope and pray that the invocation will rise within the incantations of the people of this land."

The priest opened the door and stood at the precipice. He turned and announced, "We will have Mass tonight. We must spread the word throughout the area." He then turned to TJ and asked, "Can the bell be used to summon?"

TJ responded, "Why, yes."

"Good. It will serve as the maiden's cry for all to hear."

TJ gathered and prepared his men for the anticipated event, much like a groom assembling his groomsmen. Yaz hoisted one of the children onto his shoulders at the designated time to unhitch the looped rope from under the cupola. As the sun lowered to the horizon's edge of the water, a resounding bell rang three times every five minutes. A final reverberating flurry at full hour bellowed seven times.

As the priest readied for worship, locals brought blooming chrysanthemums and placed them along the pathway to the church doors. A sign in Japanese was seen just outside the entrance which translated, *The Holy Sacrifice of the Mass. All are welcome.* Fr. Raphael waited for the church to fill. A small boy was signaled to light a dish of fragrant incense in the center of the building, under the bell tower. A waft of cherry blossoms filled the entire space, radiating outward from the aisle.

The ceremony began with a procession through the church

doors beginning with a nun. She struggled to hold the heavy processional cross vertical. A psalm echoed from Celebrant Raphael's lips as he followed behind. After giving reverence at the altar, all were greeted in the Japanese. They followed the direction of the priest as if he were teaching proper etiquette and worship protocol. TJ and crew followed in suit after the congregation. The passionate words and solemn presence of the priest in his vestments transfixed the attendees. During the culmination of the Eucharist, all instinctively bowed to the elevation of the sacred consecration. TJ, being Catholic, kneeled during this part of the service, as well as some of the crew. It was then that Fr. Raphael approached them as the designated faithful in the sign for Holy Communion. Finally, before dismissal, a blessing was given and the sign of the cross was illustrated, practiced, and repeated for the locals. Fr. Raphael instructed the nun with the recessional cross to then proceed to exit down the main aisle.

Finally, the young boy loosened the bell tower rope. Glad for this privilege, he jumped up to hang on and used his weight to bob up and down. The bell gonged nonstop to signify Mass' end. The priest turned to greet all once outside, making a point to bless all the children and babes. Behind him stood the nun handing out rosaries, holy cards, and small crucifixes. The lieutenant angled his way to her to receive a gift. She bowed and gave him a holy card. As he walked away, his men gathered in a squad huddle to see what it said. TJ turned the card to see a colored-pencil sketch of St. Francis Xavier carrying a flaming heart, a lily, and a crucifix. It read, *Apostle of Japan, canonized in 1622.* TJ remarked, "Huh, to think I was born three hundred years later and now I'm standing here as well." He stuck it in his wallet.

Following, the locals invited the priest and crew over to a portside shanty for sashimi, rice, and soba. Fr. Raphael joined in the festivities. The locals put on a puppet show of stringed marionettes in kimonos. The expressive geisha dolls and samurai warrior characters danced to the rhythm of a three-stringed instrument being plucked in the background. Huggins asked Takamatsu what this unfamiliar instrument was. Takamatsu responded, "*Shamisen* is a three-stringed instrument. It represents the three of nature, human, and ancestry together. It is to remind us of our journey in life. It originated in Okinawa." He continued, "Was that not the last place you came from?"

Huggins angrily bit his lip. He then spouted, "Well, the last place I came from was Mass. Of course, if you'd gone, you would know of the real Trinity … the Father, Son, and Holy Ghost!" Huggins confronted him to display the sign of the cross to him. Takamatsu responded with a gestured bow.

The crew admired the skill and technique of an older geisha present. Despite her age she was still poised in her abilities to perform. As she played to the puppetry, the lieutenant thought of the USO entertainment on the cruiser ships at sea. This memory was reflected too in the men. Diversions such as these had provided some fleeting creature comforts during the past echoes of conflict. The lieutenant walked over to the private and said, "Pretty far from home, aren't we?" Huggins replied, "I guess this is their comfort. Maybe all we can hope for is the best of circumstances. My comfort is the hope that we get back home from here."

Just then, Yaz tipped his head back to the sky and sniffed the air like a dog. Then he turned to the lieutenant. "You smell that?" The lieutenant took a deep breath through his nostrils and responded, "It smells like smoke from a campfire." They spun around simultaneously and saw a fire blazing through the cupola bell tower. The lieutenant shouted, "Fire! All hands to the church!"

The crew and locals dipped whatever containers they could carry into the mouth of the harbor sea. They ran as fast as they could, jostling most of the water out in haste. It was not to be. The attack on the benevolent structure could not be quenched. They began to back away from the timbers, now touched ablaze. The hotness within the church propelled glowing embers through the cupola and illuminated the cross. It proved impossible to enter through the doors of the church; once opened, the oxygen swept in to fuel the fire even more. The insulation inside due to the thickness of the thatch roof drove the smoke into the churchyard. The rescuers scampered from the scene in coughing fits.

Finally, the lieutenant ordered his crew and the locals to back away. The slow burning fuels of the magnificent pine pillars and beams ignited the thick exterior thatch, exploding into the opened sky like channeled fireworks for the islanders to view. In a mystical way, it was magnificent to watch as if in a celebrated finale.

Unexpectedly, Yaz scurried up to the lieutenant and told him, "Sir, no one has seen Fr. Raphael." The lieutenant commanded his crew, "Disperse amongst the grounds. The priest is missing. Find him."

They searched for over an hour and the priest could not be found. The lieutenant retreated back to the harbor where he had seen him last during the local festivities. He scoured the grounds, but to no avail. In a last ditch effort, he peered off of port harbor and saw a glimpse of a small fishing boat. A man could be seen sitting at the bow. TJ inched closer along the shoreline. He began to see the silhouette of a long dark coat.

He yelled out, "Fr. Raphael! Is that you?"

With a pause and despondent voice, a voice replied, "It is I."

Immediately the lieutenant removed his shoes and socks and waded out into the deep water. He beckoned and called, "Throw me a line." The priest stood up and tossed out a braided docking rope. TJ retrieved it and pulled the small craft towards him. He boarded from the side. He found the priest exasperated. TJ asked, "Are you all right?"

Fr. Raphael low-spiritedly replied, "Yes."

TJ resumed, "Do you know what happened?"

"All that I can figure, is the small boy ..." He paused. "Everything happened the way it was supposed to. However, I have been reflecting. When we left the church to join the festivities, the incense must have still been burning. The last person in there was the boy pulling on the bell. It could only be the rope left dangling from the bell to the floor that could spark such an incident." Fr. Raphael sighed and then spoke into the night sky, "The Holy Sacrifice of Mass, indeed, became the Holy Sacrifice."

The morning came all too soon. The rising crimson sun displayed the remaining aftermath. All that existed seemed to be ash piled upon ash.

The laborers and locals began sweeping and cleaning up. They retrieved the grounded casted bell. It still sat fiery hot upon the burned-out wooden embers. The gong was intertwined within the scoffed bamboo, sitting on top of the cypress altar. Remarkably, the altar surface and its supportive legs were unscathed. It had been insulated by fallen debris.

Fr. Raphael was summoned and whisked to the site. He seemed relieved to see the altar still intact and viewed it as an omen. He stated to the crew, workers, and locals, "This is a sign of our testimony!" He spoke further, "We will rise, like our Savior before us. Remember that faith will be tested. Our faith is alive in this dust and ashes. We will build once again." As Fr. Raphael moved amongst the rubble, the lieutenant joined him in his walk. Quiet to his presence, the priest only said, "I have a gift for you. Come to my quarters in an hour." He strolled away quietly on the scorched grounds.

TJ showed up to the priest's quarter and knocked on the door. He followed with subsequent knocks when they were not answered. Concerned, he walked around to the back and saw two chairs. The priest was in one. Startled, he looked up. "Oh, yes. Sit and have some tea with me." He went on to say, "You came here and accomplished a new beginning for these people through my instruction. You have served me well. Please drink." TJ was not fond of the drink, as must have slipped the good father's mind. The priest remembered then and chuckled, "Oh, I have forgotten. Next time some sugar, lemon, and ice." He went on, "I have the given authority to relieve you of any further duties here. In the time you have left, travel amongst the people here and see their country. It may surprise you."

TJ was surprised with his statement. Only an appropriate military chain of command could give such an order. The priest continued, "Not to worry, Lieutenant, I once was a commander as well." He then reached down under his chair and pulled out a kanto sword in sheath. "I have no need of this and I want you to have it. It will remind you of the sword carried by many a good man." He added, "For the Japanese, the sword is the code to heaven and to hell. Many a saint once carried them here." He sighed. "It is not so different from the oath and duty to the Marine Corps. What you carry in your belt is a symbolic reminder of what you carry in your mind and heart. Loyalty and honor are the same to both countries." He reached out to hand it to the young man. He spoke again. "In the occasions of self-respect and responsibility, you have carried it well. Much like in old feudal Japan, it was worn by the samurai class." He paused briefly and leaned in. "Remember, bear not the sword in vain. The best won victory is that obtained without the shedding of blood. The ultimate ideal of knighthood is peace." He stood up and blessed the lieutenant. "Go, now, in peace."

TJ was unable to react. He had no idea what to say. Somehow thanks were inadequate. Instinctively, he bowed to the priest. The gesture was returned. Nothing more was said.

TJ became aware that an unanticipated opportunity had opened up for him. A new stage of his journey was in order. An unfamiliar world once poised as adversary summoned him now to adventure. He had enlisted for three years and a reprieve was handed to him for the next six months. How would he begin?

Feeling some trepidation, he followed his dutiful sense of conviction to verify his new status. He called upon the United States Pacific Fleet Command to affirm the leave. Commander Henderson was now in charge of the Kyushu prefecture repatriation. On the line, he presented himself as command officer to officer. Surprisingly, Henderson himself took the call. He replied, "Oh yes, Berringer." He continued, "Up there with MacArthur." He paused. "I've heard of you, Lieutenant. You should be so privileged."

X

He was now an off-duty officer. However, TJ was reluctant to go on his leave without some Japanese-speaking person at his side. His first thought was of Yaz, who was mostly fluent in the language and industrious in survival skills, if required. The orders were approved.

TJ requested his locker box be kept in storage at the naval center in Sasebo. He wanted to secure it himself at the base to guarantee its safekeeping until his return, so he brought the box to the new security zone. As he entered into the new naval district, he suddenly heard a shout from a ship's bridge: "Hey, who let the marine in?" The lieutenant glanced above and saw a familiar smile. It was Art.

The old friends' faces brightened at seeing each other once again. Art blurted out, "I hear you are building churches now? How about one for me?" He laughed from the balustrade. They scheduled a time aside for a lunch in the officer's hall later that day. TJ proceeded to lock his box in the secured section of the base. He had no doubt in the belief that he would return.

Upon entering the hall he beheld Art in a sparkling officer's uniform. "Wow," remarked TJ, "you have been busy climbing a ladder!"

"Yes, sir," saluted Art. "The navy is quick to hand out stars when no one wants them!"

It was impressive. Like TJ, Art had enlisted in 1942. Because of his education, the navy had ranked him as a captain. He was never afraid to get his hands dirty, sporting a characteristic upbeat and quirky attitude. The navy was perceptive enough to see this, especially as it inspired the men. Now he had been escalated to rear admiral.

"Trust me TJ, I am not without my mistakes," Art continued. "The biggest is when command kept asking me to do more! Like a fool, I accepted!"

They laughed together. Art and TJ somehow knew their long friendship all the way from grade school could survive anything. It would not take much for their instinctive, synergistic wit to pick up whenever they left off. It did not surprise TJ that the armed forces needed a typhoon like him most during the conflict.

They covered the usual topic of letters sent to and from back home. Art mentioned that he had sent a ring to Adeline as a proposal in the mail. TJ said, "Wow, how did that go?" Without skipping a beat, Art responded, "I don't know, I haven't heard back. I think someone might've got off a letter before me!" They laughed again. He added, "Heard from Helen?" TJ responded, "Yes, but maybe I need to take a page out of your book!"

They continued reminiscing late into the afternoon. Art, having the commissioned privileges status, could order almost anything to eat. TJ could not believe that even bratwurst and corn on the cob was served. After dining, strawberry ice cream, iced tea, and American cigarettes complemented their satiation. It was a meal the two would long remember.

In 1930s Milwaukee, Art and TJ were raised without privilege. They met through paper routes. Art was particularly belittled as a child with his Polish last name. Fortunately, TJ became a staunch defender of him in the schoolyard. It was inevitable they would share a mutual faith. They had each other's backs in just about everything, from covering delivery routes when the other was sick to swapping altar boy obligations. Even their sweetheart gals went back to grade school and were best of friends. They seemed destined to be a part of unfolding history.

Suddenly, the loudspeaker crackled aloud: "Admiral Zimmer, please report to the bridge."

"Well," he said to TJ, "I better report or I might lose my walk of fame star!" They both stood up and Art acknowledged, "You did a really great thing here with the faith. I am not sure I could have done it. You deserve a rank above me." He paused and gleaned a smile. "Maybe best keep that between you and the big guy!" They shook forearms and saluted. Art walked away and tossed his cigarette to stomp on. Then he abruptly turned back to say, "Oh, good luck! Enjoy that furlough. And don't worry about me here … Every day's a furlough."

XI

TJ met up with Yaz back at camp quarters. He could see the cleanup from the church was already done. The bell was polished and glistening again. The altar was covered with military tarp, as if waiting for its new house. He briefly paused to take in the moment. The experiences, challenges, and revelations in his life perpetually required him to bootstrap up, despite the stakes and sacrifices that accompanied them. He noticed his reflection off the church bell. It seemed to mirror his iron-clad determination and faith to someway transform this alien land. He gathered his duffle bag, maps, and supplies, slung them over his shoulder, and met Yaz at camp opening. "Ready?" the lieutenant asked. "Let's go."

On the main island, the American repatriating ground presence was best known for their distinctive single-star Jeeps. The vehicle could handle most any terrain, including rutted and makeshift roads. Most main roads had grooved tracks from the carts struggling through the wet seasons' muddied conditions. The off-road Jeep allowed insight into Japan's magnificent archipelago of volcanic islands wrapped around turbulent seas. TJ and Yaz were on a journey to traverse them.

They set a course from the far western end of the Kyushu prefecture to the eastern breadth of Honshu. First, they would have to cross the narrow straits between the islands. At the crossing lay a small city known for its heavy steel production.

Kokura was already familiar to them through study of the military strategic manuals. It had been a targeted site for a first atomic drop in the event that Hiroshima was cloud-covered. It was saved a second time by its own cloud cover, making way for Nagasaki's unfortunate demise. The two companions wheeled into the strait between the two prefectures from above. Dormant steel plants and towers reached up from the lowlands below. They briefly stopped to take a picture of a makeshift sign which spelled the city's name in English. As they entered the city, a castle-like structure stood in front of them as if from another era. The towering square fortification of wood and stone stood stark and stolid. Encircling it was a tranquil moat where large golden carp swam, and scattered through the adjacent pond were floating lotus. Present were pitched-up gables which TJ had previously experienced during the construction of the church in Sasebo. As they got close, the large stones seemed symmetrically stacked high in a pyramid form rising out of the water. It encased the foundational wooden structure. To an enemy, the moat and stone monolith base had to be an unwelcome entry, even apart from the possibility of being plummeted with loose rock from on high.

However, it seemed eerily abandoned. It sat dormant like a dinosaur artifact from the distant past. TJ and Yaz parked and walked the gravel pathway to the imposing grand split timber door, watching out for any riffraff. TJ pulled back on the thick ring handle and the weighty door slowly opened. They could see the timber ceiling beams inside with a steep set of stairs leading to upper floors. Yaz called loudly, *"Ohayo (good morning* in Japanese)!" There was no answer. The two proceeded carefully up the precarious steps, utilizing the handrails so as not to fall backwards. Multiple times they hit their heads on low eaves as the clearance was set for residents under six feet.

Each floor was empty. Natural lighting spilled in from the wide, slotted external frames which afforded panoramic views all around. When they got to the sixth floor, the uppermost chamber, they were funneled into a circular opening. Here they viewed the breadth of the rivers, seas, terrain changes, and distant mountains. It was quite the lookout for any questionable movement abroad, as well as predictable weather changes. They discovered wood chests placed between each of the windows. They looked to see what might be stored in them and they discovered shells, ammunition, and iron ore. They seemed readied to be cast out to the ground below or launched afar. Designed within the roof hip tiles, numerous giant scaled fish faced them with mouths open—a haunting image, as if they were to swallow anything in flight. The castle fortress appeared abandoned, aged from its historical might. Being emptied, its grand inability left it defenseless.

As they exited the edifice, they could see the bustling of builders and workers in the streets not far off. There was the usual fare of street shanty food. Reconstruction of buildings from the war's bombing air raids took notice. They grabbed a bento box of primary rice, seasonal eel, soba noodles, fermented ginger, and fresh wasabi and they ate off the curb near the Jeep. The green vehicle with its white star caught the occasional glance as the locals traversed the streets, busied with their trades. Yaz occasionally spoke up to passersby, saying, "*Konnichiwa* (meaning *how do you do*)." One man with a child stopped briefly to say, "*Taihen, arigato!*" TJ said to Yaz, "Hey, I know that means thank you." However, he did not know the word *taihen*. Yaz explained that the Japanese word meant "awfully." TJ looked surprised. Yaz went on to say, "It is taken for meaning, very grateful for the Americans."

The troops supplied and helped with the rebuilding of the cities so damaged during the years of war. From perusing his manual TJ remembered Japan's war with Korea and China. All of this had taxed their resources as well.

Yaz went on, "The Japanese have always followed the emperor's mandates for the country. They were instructed to give everything of themselves for the cause. Even children were expected to assist in any way they could when tragedy struck an area. They would fetch water, weapons, supplies, rags, and medicines to manage the afflicted."

Looking around, TJ also noted the women were wearing kimonos. They stayed at a distance behind the accompanying man when walking. He asked Yaz if he knew of the ritual. Yaz replied, "That is their way of showing respect for the patriarch. The women follow anywhere they lead." He continued, "In turn, he would provide in any fashion for the whole of the family and their traditions."

TJ walked from stall to stall, inciting English *hellos* from a few. Occasionally, the locals would bow down to say "Good day" or "How are you?" Books were traded and seemed to be in plentiful supply. On one occasion, the lieutenant noticed many were looking at a particular book before they spoke to him. TJ gestured to see it. On the cover it read *Anglo-Japanese Conversation Manual*. It was dated 1945. It seemed the fad for learning English was gripping the country. It was reassuring to TJ that indeed the war was over and Japan was entering a brighter phase.

However, Western attire was far from the standard. He glanced to the side into a stall, to see a woman being draped in twisting cloth as he had seen others on the street garbed. Her face was white as snow and her hair was layered into a high upsweep, looking regal and grander than her stature itself. He stepped closer. He could see the pattern of cranes on her garment. An outline of Mount Fuji and coastal waves were brocaded into the design. The reflective shine of the material revealed it to be silk. He observed bolts of the material in a pile. He picked some pieces and opened them up. They ended up being a single cut which draped in a long T-shaped fashion, falling to TJ's ankle. It flared with obtuse wide sleeves and strict collar for the neck.

Intrigued by the process of how the garment was donned, TJ cast his eyes back to the woman and the kimono dresser, observing. The dresser had the woman stand with arms flared apart. The wrap began left to right around the body so that slack was diminished. Then a sash was tied at the back with tension. TJ noticed the woman's socks had one large toe slot as she slipped her feet into elevated wood-grain platform sandals. Her increased height and the garment's distance from the floor allowed a channel for pooling ground water to stream through and around her feet. She clacked away and briefly stopped to engage an umbrella as if expecting rain. A hand fan was fluttered open. Finally, TJ noticed a suitor waiting. The man stepped in front of her and she followed him at a distance.

Curiously, he tracked them from afar to see where they were going. As they turned a corner, they disappeared into a merchant-type tenement. From the streetscape, he observed how unseparated the living spaces and shops were. Each fitted tightly to the other. He followed the couple's entry into a dwelling, first with stepping out of their shoes and then sliding away a doorway. A stone basin was inside. He peered in subtly to see them ritually purifying themselves. A water-filled bamboo ladle tipped over their hands and then they reached to rinse their mouths as well. A metal disk with turned rim was struck, giving a resonant sound that carried through the walls. Another woman in geisha apparel appeared with two ceramic cups, a tea caddy, and square-shaped confections. Suddenly TJ recalled his similar experience with Fr. Raphael's preparation ceremony of sorts in Nagasaki. The green powder tea was carefully scooped and whisked into the hot steamed liquid. The geisha bowed and presented the tray in front of the man and woman. Finally, she took her place to sit quietly in the corner of the room while the couple slowly sipped. They practiced the ritual as if to cherish every part of the sensory experience. Though faced with a scene so unfamiliar to him, TJ felt he was witnessing a common ceremonial rite of a long venerated tradition. This was more than just sustenance for existence.

He meandered to the next structural space and noticed it was unoccupied. He stooped to peer ever so closely at the contents inside. The mere insufficiencies of the living conditions evidenced took on another meaning for him; it seemed the basics were organized by efficiency to optimize the space and uses of the dwelling. He began to see the common theme of all the tenements: The vast society lived, worked, and shared a collaborative existence here. The common areas looked like narrow alleyways with termed signs called *roji*. Children gathered and ran from storefront to storefront in a sort of game of hide-and-seek. A network of gutters aligned around dwellings to catch rain, serving like an aqueduct for fresh water to drink. The gutters contained side siphons to nourish plant and flower groves. Even an angled spill-off for clothes washing was utilized. Objects on top of doorways and under roof hangs ranged from dried orange peels to garlic and mushrooms, whose distinctive and odoriferous smells kept bugs or rodents at bay. They were also displayed for medicinal use and starches for clothes stiffening. He observed a pump well of cast iron at the end of the alley. A moistened cotton bag was placed around the spout as if to sieve out debris.

TJ went up to two wooden boxes, eager to know their use. He flipped the lids to expose recycled crushed metal cannery in one. He flipped another to discover excess grinds of fruit and vegetables composting. The lieutenant was impressed with these collective efforts to utilize resources and keep cleanliness a priority in such a densely populated area.

Most different were the doors. Nothing swung open. The wall construction hid the doors in pockets when opened—it was almost like they got in the way of living space and trade. Alternatively, many doors also coiled up and down to indicate business activity.

In the tenement, children gathered around for the sweets, a

story, or show-and-tell event of the day. Unobtrusively, he caught sight of the delights of homemade candies, toys, card games, and spinning tops.

The dwellings' interiors were truly multi-purpose. The kitchen would spring into place with sliding table and sink. The transformation of living space into sleep quarters could also be displayed. During the day, the family would sit on rolled futons, using charcoal for heating in the center of the floor. Cooking stations with an overhead slide in the roof for smoke release were common. At night the table would be folded back and the futons spread flat for sleep. As TJ stepped away from the residences, he could see that the homes shared a long building with one contiguous roof. Every three meters would be walls of separation. It struck him how quiet each dwelling was, considering the density of people who lived there.

As he rounded the corner, he spotted Yaz. Yaz excitedly spoke to him. "I met a girl. She invited us to come to her home for a meal."

TJ responded, "You met a girl? A Japanese girl? What's up with that?"

"Well, she was impressed with my Japanese and I likewise with her English."

The lieutenant gave him a look of doubt.

"Besides, the war is over and I'm free."

TJ replied hesitantly, "Yes, I suppose you are."

Yaz led him not far from where they had met. They passed through a tori gate where they were struck by incense smoke flavoring the air with cherry fragrance. Yaz came to the front of a host of nondescript dwellings. The many sliding pocket doors were now familiar to the lieutenant. Yaz declared, "Yes, this is the one." He went on, "She said a lotus gold cloth *hari-ita* (a kimono taken apart at the seams) would be hanging from the door."

They both stood in front of the simple-looking tenement. At the door entrance were two sets of *getas*, which were wooden shoes. TJ could not but notice the ikebana with one flower, one cedar needle, and one leaf directionally pointing up the step. They could see a shadow through the thick paper door moving closer, then the door channel and grooved wood bottom slid stiffly open. A bow began before a human profile came into view. A kon-nichiwa was expressed. Then, "Welcome, my name is Aya."

She was a simple girl with a porcelain face and jettison black silk hair. It wafted high toward the back, as typically seen. She stepped back with head slightly tilted down and a contemplative half smile as she urged, "Please take off your shoes and come in." She nodded to an older woman and small boy. Yaz said to TJ, "This is her guardian and her brother." They bowed without offering their names.

"Come and sit," the girl followed. "We have tea and confections." TJ began to think that the main diet of this part of Japan was tea and sweet bean biscuits.

They sat on small round cushions. TJ glanced around the dwelling, noticing more nuances of its unique character. A ceramic *neko* cat with raised paw inside the doorway reflected good nature and reassured atmosphere. On a high shelf he spied a small orange tori gate. It reminded him of entering into the port of Sasebo. He inquired from Aya, "What is that gate above?" She responded, "It is our Inari." She paused. "It is dedicated to our Shinto god of rice. The god of prosperity, harvest, and what we are given to eat."

TJ remained silent. He curiously inspected the wall containing shelves and hangings of earthenware pots, wooden buckets, pestles, and boxes. He also noticed a kitchen sink basin made of wood. Notably, the floor area was a step lower than the threshold, as if constructed for subservience to the dwelling. The women began to prepare and squat at the stove, wafting steam and charcoal smell throughout the air. The small boy climbed wooden pegs on the wall toward a hanging rope. He pulled on it to open a roof window, letting the smoke out and light in. The smell of rice, curry, and smoked fish soon intoxicated the room. "Ah," TJ breathed out to sound. "We are going to have a meal."

They brought box trays with bowls to the low table. On top was a steaming cup of ramen topped with green onion, seaweed, and hardboiled egg. Next to it, battered fish known as tempura. It was served with soy sauce, ginger, radish, and spices. A mixed bowl of sticky rice and curried meats with vegetables followed.

The men were ready to scarf in delight. Yet, they could see no utensils. TJ looked around in dismay. Suddenly, *"Ie, bako"* (meaning *no, box*) blurted from the boy, accompanied by a motion to the box underneath as if to pull something out. Sure enough, the box contained trays with chopsticks, utensils, and cloths for wiping their fingers. The men brought the bowls up to their mouths and began to master the art of slurping. Burping was a sign of a worthy meal. It was something TJ could not find in himself to do, but Yaz made up for it. TJ uttered, "It must be the tradition here. What do you say, Yaz?" Yaz replied, "Much like on the reservation, it is believed here that the meals that nourish will always produce a bodily response to the delight. It moves through you and out of you." TJ smiled. He had forgotten Yaz was a Navajo for a moment. In fact, his last name was Yazzie. The men called him Yaz for short. No one ever asked if he had a first name. They assumed it was all one. TJ then realized that Yaz probably had more in common with the customs of imperialism then the customs of puritanism. He mused on the United States' historical occupation of native America and the drive of its people to reservations. It was not TJ's chapter, but a chapter he was well aware of nonetheless. He reached across and placed his hand on Yaz's shoulder. "Thanks," he said. Yaz responded, "Thanks for what?" TJ replied, "Thanks for being here."

They finished and prepared to leave. TJ said his *arigato* and stepped out. Yaz paused and gestured he would be out in a moment. When he opened the door, the young woman and Navajo bowed to each other, speaking in words unfamiliar to TJ's ears.

As they walked away, TJ said, "That was great!" He followed, "It seems you were asking something of her at the end. May I ask?" Yaz said, "She and her family wish us well and …." "And what?" TJ curtly interrupted. Hesitantly, Yaz replied, "And the bathroom is down this alleyway."

Waiting outside, the small boy who was Aya's brother appeared with an empty rickshaw. He nodded towards them, indicating to get in. TJ said, "What is your name and how old are you?" The boy shyly responded, "Ko," and displayed his age with twelve fingers. The men stepped between the rails. Ko picked up the cart and they fell back into the seats. Ko hustled through the alleyway of the downtown streets. When he passed a round wooden building and halted, he exclaimed, "*Sumo, sumo!*" The men were somewhat startled. This must be the locals' after-dinner tradition, they thought. They climbed out and tipped the boy with an American coin. Upon entering the arena, the noise swelled with a stadium crowd. They caught sight of a Michelin-Manned center ring.

They had heard of this traditional form of full-contact wrestling but not thought it a sacred ritual. Various oversized men with loincloths bowing to each other and tossing white sand particles into the air. Bull-stomping both feet as if to drive the sand into the ground before making a run at each other. Two were summoned at a time by a robed referee waving a fan and chanting the rules of engagement. They positioned themselves diametrically, their readiness indicated by a deep squat. Then the referee's arm dropped. The wrestlers threw themselves at each other like two bulging water balloons about to collide. They meshed into each other's body folds and grabbed hold of any redundant tissue present, often looking like one whole with two heads sticking into the air. Loud cries filled the air from the crowds. One attempting to pick up the other looked like he was lifting a rubber raft filled with Jello. Grabbing for the positioned lob seemed key. Finally, one would obtain enough leverage with holds and shifting his body weight. A lift, spin, and twirl often did the trick, and the loser would be sloppily jousted from the ring. The match often lasted mere seconds.

Fans thundered cheers to honor the victor. The champ would deep-squat with folded arms in approval. Then another match would begin. TJ commented, "Look! A smaller guy is matched against another much larger." Yaz replied, "Yes, maybe we will see a little ability take out a greater inability."

After the event, TJ and Yaz exited to see Ko waiting where he had dropped them off. This time Aya was with him. Ko asked simply, "You like?"

The men nodded. Seeing that Yaz smiled and gazed long at Aya, TJ interjected, "What started this sport?"

Aya gently answered. "Sumo is a religious sport. It goes far back into our ancestry. During feudal times, the men would wake up before sunrise. For fifteen days they would train until noon on an empty stomach. Each would challenge the skill and agility of the other men to control a space. It was hard work for the body and mind. In the end, the sumo would replenish their bodies in full, just as they had given their full in training."

"What do they eat to make them so big?"

She replied, "*Chanko*. It is a high-protein stew of fish and meat. It is also stocked with vitamins, vegetables, egg, noodles, and rice."

"Why the white sand and the trampling in the ring?"

"It is salt that is thrown into the ring to purify it. They stomp to get rid of any bad spirits."

TJ questioned on. "And why the colorful robe and fan for the referee?"

"The robe shows rank and nobility. The fan is used to point out the winner." Because of his interest she continued, "The top winner is called *Yokozuna*. It is considered a god in Japan."

Yaz quickly interjected, "So they are not considered fat?"

"No," she said, "they eat because of their training to be strong and dominant in the ring."

TJ gave his two cents. "I think I'll stick with baseball."

Ko perked up and cried, "You must show me sometime!"

TJ smiled. "If you have a ball, stick, and park, I can show you."

Ko and Aya began to pick up the rails of the rickshaw. Yaz jumped in and took the rail from Aya and helped her into the seat next to TJ, and then Ko and Yaz then hurried their riders toward the tenement.

On the way, they passed the Jeep. TJ shouted, "Stop!" He was glad to see his transportation well intact. As he got out and excused himself, Ko turned toward him and said, "You show me baseball tomorrow?" He pointed across the street. "I am beginning my craft there." TJ observed a coppersmith workshop with brassware in the window. "Is this where you go to school?" he remarked. "No, I no longer go to school. I am now an apprentice," responded the boy.

Yaz was speaking to Aya quietly. Finally he nodded to her politely and joined TJ in the Jeep. The two took off to Kokura base. In the rearview mirror, TJ observed that the two stood watching as the Jeep motored out of sight. "Quite the evening, eh?" remarked TJ. Yaz replied in kind, "Quite the evening."

XII

The next morning TJ got up for his run. He decided to run along the beach. Within minutes, he drifted into the runner's zone. The morning fog mystically rose to burn off in the day's growing heat, outlining the city. It was his longest run yet. He snaked around the many steel stacks. Once he took a breather for a moment to observe metal rails running into the water. They were guide rails positioned as if to launch something. TJ noted that they fed from a factory building. He went up to the structure and viewed an entrance door. It was padlocked, so he made his way around to the back. He took notice of a piece of metal siding bent away. Looking around to be safe, he decided to take a peek. He squeezed and shimmied his way through the siding, then dusted off and stood up to take a look. Easily a dozen imperial submarines were in view, each pristine.

Much like the one that surfaced and surprised him in the Pacific waters, these had the designated numbers 1-201 on the hull sides. TJ knew what those numbers meant. His past military debriefing covered Japan's potential for creating a new vessel for deployment. In fact the Japanese and Germans were jointly working on a revolutionary long-distance attack submarine.

Here they were. They had an unusual appearance. He reached for a touch. A rubber coating was baked onto the hull, no doubt to aid in sound reduction, he deduced. He stepped back and could see the profile of channeled sleekness. It displayed amphibious aerodynamics, including acute dive hydroplaning along the frame. At the stern, an exposed compartment exhibited the marine engine. It was both diesel and electric. He had not known of or seen one until today. The brass fittings and tooling were compact and precise. A steel plate read: *20 knots peak, combined 5000 horsepower, 15000 nautical miles.*

TJ wished Art was here. He remembered him discussing "our underwater boys" machines. They could do ten knots when submerged and housed a 2,500-horsepower single diesel for 7,500 miles.

It was 12,000 nautical miles round trip from here to Los Angeles. The Japanese and Germans had advanced a combined electric and diesel motor into a single-drive system. With superb speed, diving capabilities, and long-endurance missions, it could have been a fearsome opponent. It could make it to Los Angeles and back undetected. As he made his way to the bow, he further cringed. The armament included double-diameter torpedo tubes seated in pairs with two launchers on each hull side. There was ten reloads for each chamber. He hoisted himself up to see the surface deck. The payload included retractable anti-aircraft cannons concealed into the hull. TJ shook his head. He knew his find needed to be reported.

He left through the opening he had found and resumed his jog back to the base. He found Yaz in the mess hall. He abruptly said, "We need to pack it up. We're heading back to Base Sasebo." Stunned, Yaz spoke up. "Aren't we on military leave? We got to have at least the day!" TJ paused to reason. "Okay, we can enjoy our freedom for one more day. Tomorrow we report back." Yaz sighed in relief. TJ wondered about Yaz's main interest. He suspected that the private's desire to delay was due to his curiosity in Aya. He wished to make it back to her, at least for one last time. TJ rationalized the delay for the sake of the first Japanese cooking he actually liked.

They jumped into the Jeep and made their way back into the neighborhood. As they arrived at the tenement, they saw the rickshaw in front of the door. Out came Ko before they could knock. Ko excitedly greeted them. "You come to show me baseball? I have ball at my master's shop. You come?" TJ paused for a moment and looked at Yaz. Yaz took advantage of the opportunity to offer, "You go. I will stay." It seemed the right thing to do, since TJ appreciated the recent hospitality. Ko grabbed the rails and TJ obliged to the ride.

Ko raced through the streets. As he rounded the corner, TJ could hear the hammering of metal echoing between the buildings. The boy stopped and led him into the workshop where he was apprenticed. A young man with a metallic-stained apron approached him. "Hello," he said. "Welcome to our workshop." He seemed to know perfect English. TJ looked around seeing mountains of kettles, pots, and tools of copper. Young men around Ko's age were molding and beating ductile sheets of metal. As he got closer, he could see cups, saucers, ashtrays, flower vases, and bowls being formed. The greeter came from behind and spoke up. "If you are wondering, in order to be a craftsman, they finish elementary school. They reside here in the master's workshop and home. They help with household chores in exchange for learning the trade and copying the assistants. At the end of the apprenticeship, one is considered a craftsman and earns a wage." TJ responded, "Can I look at Ko's bench?" The man bowed.

TJ was led over to where Ko worked. He could see him burnishing a small top toy. He had whistles and a car displayed on his shelf like proud prizes.

TJ spoke to him. "Can I buy the car?"

"Hai," said Ko.

"It is how much?" inquired TJ.

"I not know. You first customer!" exclaimed Ko. TJ handed him a hundred yen, the equivalent of a one American dollar at the time. Ko gleamed and said, "My master will be so pleased."

TJ turned and questioned, "Where is your master?"

Ko pointed to the back. TJ walked to the back corner of the workshop. He saw a large bench. No one was there, but he observed newspapers stacked and rows of trade tools lying in an orderly fashion.

TJ was curious to know the skills of such a master craftsman. Black-and-white photos showed a young man robed in a kimono standing proudly in front of a tool and dye machine. Others pictures included a bride on her wedding day, dressed in white with a traditional coned veil and shrine behind her. TJ took notice of a long rectangular drawer on the wall behind the bench. Seeing it as unusual to be set apart in its own place, he curiously pulled on the brass knob to see the drawer's contents. Surprised by its heavy weight, he pulled harder and it slid out faster than expected. All its contents dropped. Cartridges pinged off the wood floor as if in harmony with Christmas bells ringing. The boys raced to the back and saw the display all over the floor. Quickly, they gathered up the polished ammunition and reinstated them back into the drawer while TJ nodded, feeling somewhat apologetic. He took his leave from the shop.

As he stepped out into the air, the door closed behind him. Immediately it opened again with Ko holding something behind his back. TJ took notice. Somewhat alarmed, he prepared for an unwarranted move. He declared, "Ready?"

Ko swung out a cloth-covered ball and tossed it to TJ. He then retrieved a thick bamboo pole leaning against the workshop siding. "You show me so I can learn," said the boy.

TJ was still miffed by his find at the back of the shop. He had become consciously weary of the Japanese attempts toward peaceful reconstitution against what wartime conflicts might actually reveal. With an expressive tight-lipped demeanor, he vigorously inhaled through his nose and exhaled through the corner flaps of his mouth. He sternly looked at Ko. He then pointed the boy to hurry out to the curb and prepare for a catch. He threw the makeshift cloth-covered ball. Ko caught and returned it with a smile. TJ started to loosen his shoulder up. He had not used that throwing arm for a while. The days for pitching a baseball spin had temporarily lapsed his muscle memory. Finally, he demonstrated how to hold a bat and swing with focus on the ball. TJ pitched one in and Ko swung the bat. He cracked one clear over the workshop. Ko was in shock and disbelief. So was TJ.

When they returned to Aya's house, Yaz was nowhere to be seen. The tenement was empty. Ko pointed to a green area through the alleyway as if he knew of their whereabouts. TJ made his way into the park area. He could see the rise of a pagoda with five arching wings. A stone lantern pathway led to an imposing tori. It hovered skyward as if serving to guard a presence in the area.

He stopped and took notice of the locals performing a strange practice. All that went under the gate paused before it first and bowed. Then they entered from the side, as if to avoid the middle path. Next, they walked to a fountain. Each took up a long handled scoop from beside it. They poured water over their right hand and then their left. The water would be taken from hand to the mouth and spat out into a trough below. It seemed a ritualistic cleansing before approaching the shrine—for that is what they would do next. In front of the shrine, a horizontal wound straw rope was suspended above the entry. It served as a pull chain. When pulled, a dull clang sounded, as if to summon attention. The local would then toss a coin into a slotted wooden tray. A long bow would follow, along with two claps. Solemn standing with hands together in a prayer-like fashion ensued. After a time, the practice concluded in another bow and clap. The locals who entered the area all proceeded in the same way.

Confident as a foreigner occupier, TJ felt he would have leave of such rituals and dispensations. He stepped nearer to the eventual shrine opening without following protocol. He peered into the depth of the structure. He hoped to witness a profound reliquary or transformative state of some sort. All he could see however was incense burning and a flowered platform of lotus and chrysanthemums. It was shrouded in a sanctuary of wood, silk, and paper streamer forms draped in an orderly way across a high table. He thought, as he had before, that there must be some hidden message behind all of it.

He stepped away and in doing so caught sight of Yaz and Aya out of the corner of his eye. A long-garmented man with a headdress was placing one of those wands with paper streamers across the shoulders of both Yaz and Aya. It looked like some sort of ceremony. As the couple rose, they bowed before the robed man and then walked away.

TJ approached them both with a "konnichiwa." They responded in like. "This seems to be a special place," TJ added.

"Oh, yes," Aya followed. "This is the center of Kokura. A place we come to from all around to take part in purification and the blessings of the Kami."

TJ thought back to Takamatsu, knowing that asking a follow-up question could raise objections to him. However, he felt welcome to speak in the presence of the two. He began, "I have heard of such." He continued, "What is this Kami you say and this ritual here?"

Aya bowed and spoke, "Kami is the divine being in Shinto."

TJ respectfully stated, "Go on."

She continued, "In Shinto tradition and worship, our ancestors are in the Kami. All sentient beings guide us to this realization."

TJ glanced at Yaz but his eyes were closed. TJ blurted, "Okay, enough for now."

Aya spoke up politely, "Yet, there is more. More to what is being seen here."

TJ interjected, "Yes, I am sure, but we have to get back." He went on, "Thank you for your kindness and hospitality while we were here."

Aya politely bowed and turned to Yaz saying, "You must go now."

The three of them walked out of the grounds toward the Jeep. As the soldiers got in, Aya asked, "Have you had something to eat?" The two simultaneously responded that they had not. The girl then reached carefully behind her back and pulled out a bamboo box tied behind her garmented kimono. She stated, "This is a bento box. It has the foods you would like for your travels back. I included the confections of pressed sweet bean and ground matcha for life and energy."

TJ started the Jeep. "Thank you. Would you like a ride?" She lowered her eyes and said, "*Ie, kekko desu.*" They took it to mean no.

The two drove off in the Jeep. TJ began telling Yaz of what he had discovered during his morning jog. He mentally mapped out the detour they would take to recover the submarines for the command in Sasebo. He turned off the main road and headed toward the beach stacks he had run along earlier.

TJ was almost giddy for Yaz to see them and confirm the find. However, he discovered he was having a one-sided conversation. He realized not a word had come from Yaz's mouth since leaving. TJ glanced over. The code talker's eyes were stone-glued to the passenger-side rear mirror. TJ paused to say, "You all right?" He repeated, "Yaz?" Silent, the Navajo's eyes remained fixated on the rear mirror. TJ said nothing more.

XIII

The shiny steel stacks were in sight. They made the turn toward the metal warehouse. They both got out and TJ led Yaz through the bent drafted siding. When they straightened up, they found the subs still at command, as if waiting for ordered deployment. Yaz finally spoke. "Geez, this is really something!"

Then something happened. The subs began to rattle as if they were being started with the most violent vibration that the men had ever heard. TJ shouted in confusion, "How can this be? No one is in the crafts and they are not in water?!" Then he looked up to see the ceiling lighting swinging from side to side. Yaz fell to the ground with his ear affixed to the soil. He stared up at TJ. Their eyes pierced into each other, knowing what was happening without speaking. They bolted to the now flapping sheet metal opening, propelling themselves forward while trying not to lose balance. They had never experienced an earthquake before. They would now.

But that was not all. No one in America knew the extent of earthquakes in Japan, much less the tsunamis. The officer's manuals did not cover them, except in the context of emergency procedures. They knew wound care, how to produce water or fire, gas masking, and handling serious light exposure. Not this.

In the ancient writings of Japan's history, the island relied on the fierceness of nature to battle against intrusive Mongols or swamp ship invaders. In its geographical position, Japanese society was naturally fortified from outside advancements and communications until the nineteenth century. It was little wonder why the Japanese honored the force and protection of nature and often spoke of it with respect. It was not until the advent of oceanographic mapping that knowledge of the ring of volcanic bursts and shifting tectonics around the island reaffirmed the contentious interplay between land and water. If the reaction occurred at sea, the entire water wavelength produced a rapid tide which overwhelmed the shoreline. The rise of water against the rise of land was a theme often symbolized in Japan's prolific art culture, specifically in paintings. After all, Fuji was the genesis of the island's majesty and character. The Japanese were accustomed to the concept of this connectedness through feeling the land's movement sometimes daily.

TJ and Yaz exited the building and ran to the Jeep. They could feel their legs weirdly moving sideways from contact with the rumbling surface. TJ jumped over a gaping split in the dirt, hoping he would not land in another. They made it to the truck and paused for a moment to orient themselves and then focus on how to proceed on four wheels. Fortunately, the tremble was subsiding.

TJ started the vehicle with the intent to get to high ground. However the scape of the road before him turned into a chasm of undulating fissures. He had to find another way out. TJ quickened his words. "Yaz! Scope the best way out!"

Yaz grabbed the binoculars and jumped down to the road to look ahead. Suddenly, he felt water rise up to his ankle. "Sir," he exclaimed, "water rising!"

TJ looked to the side and started to see the low brush disappear rapidly. The water was making quicksand of the road. Without a word, he fired up and yanked Yaz into the vehicle sideways shouting, "We have to find high ground! Makes no difference which way!" He sped away from the levels of water encroaching on the Jeep. It looked like a great hand of a wave brushing the land with a coat of silt water. TJ knew that he would have to gun it to the Kokura mountain hillside. He only hoped to outrun the rising ambush to the left and right.

Unexpectedly, Yaz yelled, "Watch out!"

TJ saw a shifting crack in the earth and swerved. He shouted back, "We are going to have to jump some of these cracks if we are going to make it. Keep an eye out so we can get through to the trees."

Yaz stood up in the Jeep and pointed to an opening up to the tree line. "Only one crack to jump, but it's big!"

TJ floored the Jeep to the opening and saw the crack in the earth up ahead. He shouted, "It looks like we are going to have to jump it! Hold on!"

As TJ raced the Jeep, he could see the water approaching from behind in the rearview mirror like a bloodhound on his heels. He fumbled into his front pocket and pulled out the rosary he carried with him always. He grasped it in his hand as he recited the Hail Mary. He pulled back on the steering column as if he was lifting up the nose of an airliner, crying, "Godspeed!!" The front wheels lost contact with the ground as the back jolted off. As they were airborne, TJ could fleetingly see and hear the gushing of water under the chassis into a newly created gorge. He murmured, "Mary, help us."

The flight seemed to last forever as the weightlessness ensued. He had no idea how long the jump was, nor did he have the will to look. Suddenly, a thump of the front wheels, followed by a rocking bump of the back tires over an edge. The Jeep spun out to the right and came to a stop. TJ looked back. The water crested and tilted over the lip of the crevasse behind. He turned the wheels straight and powered up the incline into the tall cedar trees.

They came to a safe point in elevation to see the breach of events below. Water bathed the area with floating wood, metal scraps, and tin debris. Yaz stated, "That was an earthquake?" TJ replied, "It must have happened close at sea as to rumble us. The rising water was practically on top of us." Yaz said, "Like someone dropping a big rock in a shallow pond?" TJ followed, "Yeah, something like that." He placed the rosary back in his top pocket. He could see a deep impression of the beads and crucifix in the palm of his hand.

As they gazed around the Jeep, Yaz spotted some packs and scattered supplies at the base of some tall, stoic cedars. "Sir," he gestured. "Shall we take a look?" TJ was somewhat hesitant. He had heard of uninformed renegades still at large since the surrender was not fully known or recognized by all. He unstrapped his Luger from the case and they proceeded with caution.

Yaz rummaged through the supplies to discover they were indeed Japanese military. "Look a little further," urged TJ. Yaz encountered drawings of calligraphic script. Black ink bottles with broad tip brushes accompanied the paper inscriptions. "Do you know what it says?" TJ asked.

Inspecting carefully, Yaz said, "I can only make out certain letters. It's more illustrations of some kind of shapes." He continued, "It looks like decorative art, as if someone decided to sit down and paint serene figures." He noticed worn books with stained photos of families inserted between pages. "What do the books say?" TJ asked. Yaz could only make out a word. "Bushido," he sounded. TJ looked around and saw many worn shoes displaced throughout. He could not make out whether a base camp was once out here. Nothing indicated as such except the abandoned items.

TJ motioned to step further into the forest to have a look around. Yaz streamed ahead, knowing he had the eyes and nose to sniff out most anything. They began to notice more camouflage saddle packs scattered and left throughout the grove. They proceeded more cautiously now. Yaz had a machete in hand to whack away hanging vines and any creepy crawlers landing near.

As TJ gazed upward, a quiet fog began to undulate, dampening the canopy of the cedars and pines. Moisture dripped below, nursing the thick fauna of moss, miniature oaks, and undergrowth creep on the floorscape. The vapor felt like a cleansing aquacade soaking the clothing through to the outer layer of skin.

TJ stopped and spoke. "You go further and I'll mark behind so we know our way back." He took his machete and scored an x into a line of trees every ten meters for passage back while Yaz continued on, almost out of sight. TJ knew Yaz had the military survival instincts to remain close as trained.

Without warning came a horrific cry. It came from the direction ahead, down by Yaz. TJ instinctively crouched down on alert, readying his Luger. Yaz emerged from the brush running at full speed and dashed past him with a whiteness he had never seen. TJ remained quiet and calm in his tracks. His instincts sensed Yaz was running from something rather than being pursued. Nonetheless, TJ was ready to defend his ground and cut off any action. But, nothing happened. Yaz was no longer in sight on his path back to the forest line. TJ was to make a decision: to retreat or press gingerly forward. He elected to make sense of the strange, raucous event. He proceeded up to an inclined mound and decided to creep on all fours, noting a vista clearing the view ahead. Being combat-trained, he chest-crawled to the top, keeping his head low to mesh into the forest's carpet of moss. He raised his eyes up only to see more of the same as behind him. Nothing was seen to move or pose a threat. He remembered Yaz grew up on the reservation; he had his own superstitions and probable demons to work with.

TJ rose up to his knees. He saw something shimmering as light broke through to the forest bed. Moss mounds permeated the landscape, emanating distinctive odoriferous smells. Reflective relics mirrored at the top of these. He stood and walked around observing the seamless tranquility of the area. Curious, he went up to the rounded masses holding his nose and observed the mirroring shimmer more closely. It looked like a steel point coming out from the center top of the encrusted mossy mold. He lifted his foot to a push over the heap. It uncovered its secrets.

Aghast, he stepped back. There lay the decomposing body of a human in fetal position, gripping the handle of a long knife. The shimmer he had seen on top was the cold steel exit of a kanto sword.

The bushido, as it was called, was the military code of honor and morals dating back to feudalism and the samurai oath. It was passed down generationally as a way of life, even more than as religious beliefs. It was loosely analogous to the customs of European Crusaders and their unrivaled chivalry.

TJ remembered a discussion at lunch with Art discussing the tactics of the adversary. Art routinely instructed his battleship gunners for complete obliteration of any diving Zeros. In an effort to preserve the U.S. mission, any flying metal parts, fire, and wreckage needed to be kept at bay from the decks of the brigade. The crewmen at sea would describe the act of *hara-kiri*. Art would reassure his men, "This is their ritual, not ours." He went on to surprise even the lieutenant by stating, "Pride is the deadliest of virtues. The Japanese can prove it." He then outdid himself in awarding each gunner a steak dinner if "not a speck of this waste" was seen shipside.

Art's words assured TJ of what he witnessed here. It was a part of a conscience by which he would never abide. Instead, he recommitted to the way that served him throughout his life. His faith was with him always and was reinforced as a marine. The USMC motto "semper fidelis" had a meaning deeper than ever now.

TJ found his way back by the marked trees to the Jeep. He found Yaz sitting in the vehicle shivering in his boots. TJ glanced ahead. He could see the waters in the lowlands now receding back to the ocean. He sipped from his water canister and pulled out the box of food Aya had packed for Yaz and him to eat. They ate and felt quietly reinvigorated by the meal. They waited for the right moment to see the pathway back. Just before sunset, TJ started the Jeep.

As the contours of a soaked Earth once again availed, they could see their route outlined. The Jeep steered and slid easily down from the timberline. Covered in mud, they motored through slosh that spit up debris across their bottom fatigues. They finally reached a main road. As the Jeep sputtered along, torn wood boarding and thatch roofing was spewed across the landscape, showing no footings of construct beneath. Nature's aftermath bellowed a stink. They scarf-outlawed their faces all the way back to Sasebo.

Through the haze in the sky, a deeper hue bathed the sun as it lowered to the horizon. They both stared at the round crimson color as if postured as a revealing sign from the heavens. Yaz finally spoke up. "There is an Indian saying," he sighed. "When the sun is blood red, the sacrifices of the nation show their sorrowful face."

XIV

As they drove into base, TJ was relieved to see new construction where the church once presided. Yaz saw Huggins approach and jumped out of the Jeep. Huggins exclaimed, "Did you feel the quake?" "Yeah," said Yaz, "We bronco- rode through it!"

TJ got out of the Jeep without a word. He was steadfast in his determination to relay his discovery. Heading toward the naval seaport shipyard, he saw Art's ship still docked. He went up to the security gate watch, saluted, and spoke: "I have news for the admiral, right away. I am an off-duty officer." The guard squinted at him. TJ continued, "Tell him this is past command first lieutenant of the Second Division United States Marine Corp with official news." The attendant radioed to operations. The lieutenant waited for clearance. Finally, permission came. He was escorted up to the admiral's quarters. Upon entry, instead of his usual comic wit and warm greeting, Art radiated worry.

He asked him to close the door. Art began, "Well TJ, I am leaving my command." He went on, "It seems General MacArthur wants to move on to the next strike."

"What?" TJ cried out.

"Korea," the admiral said, gazing through the cabin window. He went on, "It seems we moved into a new phase of a conflict I am finding difficulty with. It's our supposed ally Russia. They have moved into the north part of Korea in an occupational land grab. We are being asked to use our footings here to move into the south part. I see no good to come of escalating more tensions as seen in Berlin. It looks like democracy is going to butt heads with our communist conspirators." He went on, "We have done what we can here to secure operations and rebuild this part of the world. I have no interest in command any further. We have completed what our mission required. I am stepping down from this post."

TJ sat down, stunned to hear the sudden turn in events. He, too, had not anticipated another march. After all, it had seemed the war was against Japan alone. He found it difficult to stomach a prolonged stance into new terrain. Art went on to say, "We both are close to the end of our three years. I believe we will fight again, but not in this conflict." And he paused and stood in front of TJ. Art said something then that TJ thought he would never hear. "The field marshal has arrived. Let's call it and meet him."

Douglas MacArthur was the most respected and admired general in the Pacific Rim. He came from a generation of medaled men in his family. TJ had read extensively of his accomplishments. He remembered his commanding voice at sea during the invasion at Okinawa. He never heard anyone inspire as much through a rallying call of duty, honor, and country. His words sustained many troops in the worst of conflict.

They went up to the ship's bridge and caught sight of this giant of a man with commanding presence. He overlooked the bow with his characteristic corncob pipe, aviator glasses, and one foot perched upon the bridge's bottom rail. They approached him from the periphery of his eye.

"Permission to speak, General," they chorused.

"At ease," he comfortably said.

Art led, "General, we are at the end of our mission here. Sir, we'll be brief." He paused momentarily. "We secured Sasebo and peaceful repatriation efforts are ongoing. We ask for release from our completed enlisted duties to return home."

MacArthur gave them a long squint before he responded, "Men, a peace at home is always the quest to follow." He paused and carried on, "I would gladly yield every honor awarded me in war, for a line in this century's history books crediting my contribution to advancing peace."

TJ exhaled softly, "Whoa!"

The general continued, "If you two are sure of this in yourselves, I do bid you farewell."

TJ spoke now extemporaneously. "General, thank you. In this service to you and our country, we have summoned courage when we saw little in ourselves, pledged our faith in dangerous times for belief, and willed hope when hope was abandoned. It's time for our departure back to home soil."

The general put his hands on each of their shoulders. "Boys, you have done a great service and honor to your country." He shook their hands and saluted. "Godspeed."

As the two men left, they glanced back to see their field marshal looking seaward with his foot on the stoop. His imposing aura would remain with them long after their departure.

An honorable discharge suited Art and TJ very well. They had experienced different pathways that somehow had brought them together. They were to embark on their return journey in one day. TJ decided to make his way to the compound where the new church was being constructed. He saw Huggins along the way and told him the news of his immediate discharge. Huggins had enlisted for five years. He exclaimed, "They made me a sergeant, sir. New command orders will take me into South Korea in a week."

The discharged lieutenant spouted, "Congratulations, Sergeant! Well deserved!" He went on, "Oh, by the way, in your morning run, follow the jogging path that will take you to the beach head steelwork stack in Kokura. You'll find quite the prize there. You may find yourself a lieutenant soon!"

Huggins responded, "Thank you, sir."

"One last thing," TJ asked, "Have you seen Fr. Raphael hereabouts?"

"Yes," he responded, "he is harborside with the locals."

TJ made his way to the wharf. The merchants were more numerous now—notably food stores, eateries, and even a gasoline station. He caught sight of the priest sitting at a stand sampling some catch of the day. "Father, sir!" he shouted out.

The priest waved him over. "I heard you are shipping off."

TJ replied, "Word does travel fast here." He followed, "I wanted to part with good wishes." He went on, "I did not know all you have done for the cause of duty, both in the military and in the faith."

"Oh, yes," the other chuckled. "I guess I have something in common with the great Crusaders transformed through war and faith. Somehow they go hand in hand."

TJ smiled and then looked down. He paused before he spoke. "I would think you might understand something I have been carrying." He continued, "Despite my intentions to serve in my duty call both as a soldier of the Marines and as a soldier of faith, I am leaving with a heavy heart."

The priest interrupted and asked," When do you ship out?"

TJ reluctantly replied, "I leave tomorrow morning."

Fr. Raphael paused to ask, "Would you like the sacrament of reconciliation?" TJ was silent. It had been a long time. The priest continued, "Our Christ is always abundant in love and mercy."

TJ finally bowed his head and said, "Yes, Father."

The priest lifted a stole from his sack and placed it around his neck. He then lifted another and placed it around the neck of the lieutenant. They walked alone to the shoreline and stood against the outline of the forested mountains. The crew and laborers paused to watch them from afar. They knelt together with bowed heads reserved for the spiritual presence of mystical resolve.

It was before dawn when Art jostled TJ. "Rise and shine," he urged. "We have a long journey ahead." TJ showered and dressed. He promptly downed some coffee and hurried to retrieve his case from secured storage. He gave the tag to the attendee. The guard fetched it but had difficulty lifting it for the hand-off. He gasped, "What do you have in here—machine parts?!" TJ smiled and signed off for it. He met up with Art shipside.

"So, Art, what's the plan?"

Art announced in his no uncertain way, "We have to catch a tanker that will take us out to sea and hook up with a destroyer. Then it will slingshot us around Guam for due east. You ready?"

"Aye aye, Admiral," his mate scoffed.

They loaded onto the tanker. It was an empty oil barge used for operations and was void of the accommodations they were accustomed to. Nonetheless, they were glad to be at sea hoping America would be the next land mass stepped down on. As they pulled away from port, TJ grabbed his binoculars for one last look at Sasebo. He took in the transformation of a simple fishing village into a naval command center. He could see where the prison camp started and the phoenix of a church he had laid the groundwork for. At the bay point, he viewed a couple waving from the rocky point precipice jetting out toward him. He thought it a bit unusual, despite it being a universal gesture in peacetime. He put the glasses down for a moment to wipe the eyepieces clear and took a closer look. "Son of a gun," he murmured. The optics immediately dropped to his chest as he raised both arms in a high fanning flurry. It was Yaz and Aya. He stood and waved all the while. The vessel made a sweeping turn to the east. The glare of the sun overtook their images finally.

He lifted his foot up on the bottom side rail and elbow on the top, with his hand to his chin. Art came up and said, "Enjoying the ride?" TJ continued to fix his eyes on the coastline of Japan.

Art placed his foot on the same rail and looked out as well. "Looks as if you left something behind." TJ did not respond. Art paused, lit up a cigarette, and continued, "We all have left something behind, Lieutenant. Maybe we should consider that we have something to take forward."

TJ spoke. "Do you think we should have stayed longer, for duty's sake, as the general has?"

Art tossed down his cigarette and stepped to smudge it out. He replied, "As I was leaving, the general gave me a letter. I believe it will guide us for the duration of our journey." Art removed a finely creased letterhead from the inside of his jacket. He continued, "I think it's a good time to share it with you. It's short. It's handwritten from MacArthur. It should take us home."

Art handed it to TJ and stepped back into the loins of the tanker. TJ sat down on a bench. He beheld the handwriting of his chief commander, his hero. He savored the moment and then decorously slid it open as if to fulfill one last mission. The letter had no heading and contained only a quote. It read:

> *Build me a son, O Lord,*
> *Who will be strong enough to know when he is weak*
> *And brave enough to face himself when he is afraid*
> *One who will be proud and unbending in honest defeat*
> *And humble and gentle in victory.*
> *—Douglas MacArthur*

XV

Guam was the furthest island outpost for the United States, most noted as a strategic foothold in the Pacific theater. It was bombed only hours after Pearl Harbor and served as Japan's first occupied land gain. Art and TJ's tanker docked there and they boarded the cruiser to sail home. The place was uneventful now.

TJ and Art remembered the long journey to rescue Guam. After all, that was why they had gotten their deployment from California. In the history of the United States, no country had ever before occupied land on which the American flag was raised.

From the start, it was priority number one in the Pacific Rim. Most of America had no idea, as it got little mention in U.S. history texts. It received twenty-one days of bombing fury by the Allies in 1944. They required it for strategic presence and as a checkpoint against all of the Far East. At the time of conflict, Art and TJ were at sea en route to serve as the on-deck reinforcements. Now, they looked at the bombed-out island with America's flag waving on high. Art spoke. "The whole place was once a tropical paradise."

Art picked up a discarded Guam paper. He read aloud the old headline, *20,000 Japanese occupying forces finally sealed in death. Only 1,500 marines lost and 5,000 wounded. Guam retaken!* They looked and raised an eyebrow at each other. Art blurted, "Talk about dodging a bullet! If we hadn't taken it back, our B-29 with Fat Boy could never have reached its target." TJ then said, "Look, a map here says it's 3,800 miles to Hawaii! After that, smooth sailing to California!" They shared a sigh of relief. But, too soon. Nature had not yet spoken.

They had experienced the war as a test to their duty, courage, and fortitude. Now, they crossed the rim of the largest ocean, as yet ignorant of the summer season's gusts and torrents. They soon were to encounter the enduring tantrum of a tempest. The strong winds this time of year would wreak havoc. Monster swells and haphazard wave patterns would dominate the seas. In the best months, schooners relied on the favor of currents to make great time across this area. Now, the Pacific would call its own course across the limitless horizon of water. The occasional spasm of the Earth's crust would burp up an occasional island to serve as a dot marker for weaving around.

The hardest thing was the tossing of the flotilla above the water line in misdirected fashion. Occasional flops could be tolerated for a few seconds. The long-suffering crew hoped for mere minutes of relief but was kept waiting for it in the ensuing days and weeks. The food galley was little attended. Eating had no appeal during these times. The best place to open one's eyes was deckside, for a fixed view of the stable horizon.

The lifting swells soaked the howling winds and chilled even the most insulated of the men. Most retreated into the belly of the vessels. There, they were encased in an endless roller coaster, dishing out their stomach contents upside down. The persistent rocking movement back and forth from deck to cabin became the norm. Much worse, the men avoided each other's company, so not to addictively spread the endless upchucking. It was not uncommon for a man to lose twenty-five pounds of weight in one week in these torrents. The only occasional relief would come with a glass of water and lime to sustain them. When they attempted to recline in the berth, they cramped with a wrenched feeling of what they believed was like to maternal birthing.

As with all the crew, Art and TJ spent most of their effort to minimize the angst. It seemed like forever until they reached the outskirts of Hawaii. It was easy to lose touch of the day and time at sea. As the Pacific finished its frenzy, the waters smoothed toward the distant welcome site of Aloha Tower, Hawaii. The cruiser had left Japan in early August and arrived in September. No one dared mention the marathon they had just endured, as it would automatically elicit a visceral reaction. The inviting seaport harbor at Honolulu was pristine and radiant. Hawaii's backdrop skyscrapers were rising at a steady pace. America's uprising to power was showing its panache to the world.

No indication of the 1941 raid was seen except in the darkened shadow of an underwater vessel. The USS Arizona lay submerged in a bath of aqua blue, translucent and glittering in refracted light as if vigilantly waiting to resurface. The cruiser steered slowly around the sunken ship, giving its respects, then banked easterly and resumed full speed out of the harbor. Art held onto the rails next to TJ as they looked back. He remarked in his witty way, "One thing I can say, they got better sleep than us this past month." TJ shook his head with a half grin.

They had another twenty-five hundred miles to Los Angeles. The cruiser was making good time as they clipped past any signs of inclement weather on the horizon. As they got within reach of California, the offshore seas began to rumble and ruffle their smooth, gliding approach. The crew agreed to make mention to the bridge that they were not interested in a repeat ride of the past month. The bridge captain confirmed and proposed to abort Los Angeles for the smoother waters around the Baja. It would take them through Panama's canal and would add two days longer at sea. No one disapproved.

As they entered the blue waters of Baja, the sea settled less to a wave than to a mirroring of the sky. The intense sun reflected a calm serenity as it dried out their waterlogged skin. A crewmember pointed out starboard side. Spouts of sea spray surged up from the surface and drizzled the waves.

At first, TJ rubbed his eyes. He believed he was seeing aquatic submarines on patrol. The cruiser cut its engines and crawled cautiously through the disturbances. The skipper bull-horned out, "Enjoy the water show, boys!" A flipper the size of a Japanese tenement burst out above the waterline and slapped down on the bay. The crew cheered to welcome the slick mammoths of the sea breaching and frolicking carefree in front of them.

Deckside, TJ started to think of his postwar free time. The men expressed their new freedom in diving into the water in hopes to hitch onto a fin. The whales would not comply, countering with a water slap too close for comfort. TJ walked across the bow to the ship's shadowed side for some quiet. He gazed at the water. Not far away he spied a humpback breached motionlessly. He was amazed to see all the crustaceans shackled to its great body. He caught sight of its giant eye staring at him. An extended peering, as if it willed to write a manual of survival into TJ's mind. A message direct of beast to beast, survivor to survivor. For a moment, the whale drifted about in a jaded-like and uncaring state. Much like TJ, free of schedules, concerns, or worry. All too soon, the whale closed its volleyball-sized eye. The mammal rolled, stretched, and arched back down into the depths without a trace. TJ recalled one of the quotes of his farewell general: "Old soldiers never die, they just fade away."

The night's sleep was welcome. The waterway through Panama was nearing. An American engineering feat, the canal connected the two massive waters of the Pacific and Atlantic. The cruiser slowed at daybreak to enter the walled corridor. A levy locked water against water to buoy ships up and down. A serpentine isthmus remained for them to slowly navigate around the rock cliffs and tropics. The men stood along the deck rails admiring the excavated walls against the dense jungle. Art spoke up. "What a great show this is to remember from our victory lap!"

Although the canal was a mere fifty miles long, the meandering speed made it a long trip for most ships. Unexpectedly, the captain of the cruiser mandated a clothes change over the intercom. The men were instructed to change into light full-body garments and place netting over their face. They were also commanded to avoid exposure to any water pools. Art protested, "Has the captain lost his mind? It must be a hundred degrees here!" Nonetheless, they unwillingly complied.

TJ and Art were enjoying a snooze in the intense sunrays on deck cots when their confusion over the captain's command was demystified. A swarm of bandits began to buzz. A winged insect known for its light, nimble landing began its needling through whatever skin available. Soon the swatting and slapping was rampant, chorusing all over the deck.

The men referred to them as the little kamikazes. The thumb-sized mosquitos gave ample visual warning to their victims by their size alone, but their sheer numbers allowed many to commence in their bloodsucking dive. The jungle flyers would continue their assault until fought. After an insult, most men retired into the ship's belly for a good sleep, already weary from the intense sun. However, they woke the following morning with fevers and chills.

TJ had a mild case that resulted in a bad headache and diarrhea. Art felt hard though. TJ would not see him again on the deck during the voyage. When they exited into the gulf warm waters, the line to Florida was clear. They swept up and around Miami following the Florida coast. Norfolk base was within field goal range.

TJ began to worry. He had to inquire about Art. He went up

to the bridge. "With permission, Captain, I am looking for the admiral." He continued, "I can't seem to locate his whereabouts." The captain replied, "May want to look in sick bay, officer."

TJ hurried his way to the infirmary area of the ship and requested to know whether the admiral had presented. The attendant nodded. The staff requested TJ to wash up before entering. TJ walked inside to see a display of bed netting around the room. It was the first time he saw his chipper-natured and strong-willed friend in the quiet. Under a stack of blankets, his eyes were closed. TJ noticed sporadic shaking in his arms and legs. He had a wet cloth on his forehead as to temper the overheating. He stood silent at Art's side for a while with hat in hand.

A nurse came by to administer a shot and ushered him out. TJ stepped behind the net and walked to the nurse's station. The nurse returned and hesitantly spoke, "Your friend has malaria." She continued, "We have administered quinine to help. He will need to stay here until the fever has broken and he becomes healthier." TJ said, "Is there anything I can do?" The nurse replied, "It is best to leave him for now. He needs to conserve his energy." TJ pressed, "Surely I can sit at his side!" The nurse responded, "Sorry, but if you are subject to the mosquitos' infection or remain around these nets, you too will fall ill. However, we can give you an update as often as you wish."

TJ left somewhat despondent and concerned. He had not predicted this other kind of winged invasion. Art was his oldest friend. They shared the chapters of grade school through dutiful enlistment. Arrival into Norfolk was in one day. TJ could not fathom Art not standing on his two feet for their return home. He said his rosary, offering the last leg of the journey to his friend's recovery. The victory ship was cruising up the eastern coast of his homeland.

Throughout the remaining day, a cloud of sadness over took him. The burden of service, purpose, and duty was taking its toll on him.

Finally, the USS cruiser docked. TJ stepped down the ramp onto his native country's soil. He had not had the time to fully process his return to America. He was struck by the size and scale of the Norfolk base. It was the central headquarters of the United States Fleet Command since World War I. TJ stopped to count seventy-five ships, one hundred thirty-four aircraft, and eleven aircraft hangars. He summarized, "No way, no how, no one has a chance to defy us again." He was content to wait at the pier with case and sacks at his side. He would not depart for the flight to Milwaukee until the admiral disembarked.

TJ stood an hour at the base of the long ramp which connected the ship's deck to the pier. Art finally appeared. He was in a wheelchair. They gathered his belongings as the captain brought him down the long descending ramp. Art gave TJ a wink and spoke up. "Thanks for waiting. I thought I'd be popping up daisies soon on that rig!"

The lieutenant said, "Good to see you up and about, even in a four-wheeler."

Art went on, "Ah, the final leg." He paused. " ...You'll have to take it on your own." He continued, "A few more tests are needed to flush out the bug."

TJ automatically replied, "I can stay until you're ready to go."

Art smiled with an appreciative look, "No, you go, you have family waiting for you. I won't be long." They continued to wheel him by. Art raised his hand in salute. The lieutenant eyes teared as he saluted his comrade away.

He took a deep breath, then picked up his sacks and case. A ground official showed him to the aircraft gate, indicating the direct flight to Billy Mitchell Field in Milwaukee. As he walked along the strong steel hull of the class cruiser, he thought of the enduring journey of his entire mission. The flight he was about to take was bringing this time in his life to an end. At the tip of the bow, he glanced over his shoulder to look back at the airplane's sweeping, contoured bow. He stopped to notice the insignia. The letters read, USS Helena. A new chapter was about to begin.

XVI

He suddenly awoke from his deep sleep. Somewhat disoriented, he perked up in his terminal seat and refocused on his surroundings. He saw the overhang banner sign that read, *Welcome home troops to Mitchell Field*. He felt he was reliving his journey afar, foggy to whether the present was real or not.

"I am home," he sounded to reassure himself. The familiarity of Milwaukee's brewery-scented air came back to him. Yet, the reality confronted him. "Where is everyone?"

No one was there. He had started alone in his courage to step forward in service and had finished alone in his step back. He uttered aloud, "What could they understand of it?" He paused, "Is this what Art will go through? And my men?" It seemed forever he was sitting in that terminal seat in the Milwaukee airport. He was accustomed to the next command. In panic, he thought about returning to Virginia and joining Art for the next leg. "That's it," he thought. But then he stopped to press his hands on his forehead and cover his eyes. It was not the hero's return he had dreamed about. Then again, the three years had taught him to not know what to expect.

Finally, the outside doors swung open. Helen and his parents appeared. Holding onto an anticipated "Hoorah!" and "Surprise!" he waited. As they approached, he saw exasperated looks on the faces he loved. He stood up. He wanted to be certainly recognizable in all that may have changed about his person. Forlorn, his dream was dashed with the first words out of their mouths.

"Sorry, we're late. Traffic was bad."

It deflated everything for him. He felt like he was still away. Maybe morbid news of delivering a folded flag would have raised some glee. He did not know how to make sense of it all. He decided then. He would bury it deep in the smoked-out fire in his belly. He hoped in time to forget it all. For the sake of duty, it was over.

XVII

America was on the move. The new peacetime brought a culture of construction and consumption. Milwaukee was transformed with high rises, expressways, and shopping centers. Suburban appeal welcomed the lifeblood populace from urban squalor. The boom of homes and family fueled a new middle class and a new manifestation of the American dream.

TJ and Helen were wed and coasted on the wave of the boom. America was now the superpower reaping the fruits of prosperity. The GI bill provided a waft of advancements and opportunities to be taken. TJ moved from business accounting courses to a law school at his university of choice.

They captured the nation's long honeymoon bliss and started a family. The family size, house square footage, and suburban mass continued to expand. The only scare now was the occasional fallout shelter alarm which the Cold War ushered in.

Art did make it back to Milwaukee. He recovered and got into the car salesman business. No one could resist his flare and charm. In his first year, he was awarded as the best Buick salesman in the state. The two friends resumed their time together. Each looked forward to the cribbage and nickel bet poker games. The war was never discussed or even brought up between the two.

One lunch Art said, "TJ, I have another horizon in sight. A place you and I have experienced before. How does California sound?!" He excitedly carried on, "That's the place we ought to be! Can you convince your first mate?" TJ nodded uncertainly and said, "You know it will be a tough sell." Art urged, "Why, you are in life insurance now. Take it anywhere. It shouldn't be a problem!" The familiar chuckles returned.

Two months passed and Art was not around for his usual lunch dates with TJ. Finally, he received a letter with photos from the beaches of Los Angeles. Art had gotten married on the quick and convinced his Milwaukee girl they'd be better off in Beverly.

TJ showed the letter to Helen. She shook her head and said, "Thank you but any such idea is not up for discussion." TJ wrote back, "I tried for the transfer but I'm afraid I have been grounded. I'll have to sit this one out." Art followed up with a package a week later. TJ opened it and placed it on the back end of his desk. It somehow made sense of the time they never spoke about. It stirred a memory for him. His Marine chest was locked and stored away in a basement corner collecting dust. On his chest of drawers, he kept a toy car he had bought from a young Japanese boy whose name he could not remember. Art had sent the only consolation he was proud to keep on his desk. It was a plaque adorned with the phrase, *Americans never quit.* Somehow this made their distance closer.

XVIII

JR was born. He grew to develop an uncanny aptitude to construct a new order out of the one he was brought into. Before he could walk, he made a functional doghouse out of discarded empty milk cartons. From erector sets to engine building, he demonstrated a creative genius to reshape most anything he touched. During his school days, he stayed well after school to master a project or complex challenge. His attention to detail and problem solving called forth praise from his early teachers. They commented to his parents that he was destined to be a "riser" of some sort.

His physical skills served him in the extracurricular arenas. He had a throwing arm for the limelight, but instinctively played it down to attribute wins to the team skills of others. In many events he remained patient on the bench until called upon to perform. He was known for his key shots at the basketball buzzer or key passes in football to bring the team victory. Most of all, he learned to credit the team and knew that if any competitiveness existed, it was solely within himself. Innately, he stood up to any bully for the sake of the underdog or when others were mistreated—much like his father had done.

It was in high school when his character and ambitions began to bloom. He turned to a different school than TJ's alma mater. His sights were on a private education. Unfortunately, it was one his parents could not afford. But, that did not deter him. He persisted with jobs and side work that would fill his days as his studies allowed. Fundamentally shy, he sought unconventional ways of problem solving that would escape his parent's criticism, particularly if his academic performance remained strong.

He committed himself to a leadership motto: "If it's to be, it's up to me." His tenacity and confidence thrust him to the top of his class. One time, he surprised even himself by trying out for an acting role. He stunned his parents in the audience come showtime, as they had been unaware of his lead role on the stage.

The most profound thing about him was the evident influence of his Jesuit education. The adopted mindset of Ignatius's teachings, "Ad Manorem Dei Gloriam," would stand out the most. The letters AMDG would find its place under his name on every paper. It was his guidance advisor for college who would bequeath him with the label "great soul." He had a big heart open to learning and giving ever more.

Scholarships came his way to attend most any school. He stayed in his hometown to attend the university his father was at. The path to a medical profession appealed to him most. It was his sense of caring, problem solving ability, and persistence that would shape his resolve.

TJ would often say to his son, "These are your golden years! Enjoy them." However, JR did not feel like slowing down for the benefit of leisure. To him it was more work with little play, if any at all. He had to juggle his work and school life with steely-focused effort in order to pay for and exceed in it. Little time was left for anything else. TJ would label it as character building and reassured JR by saying, "One day you will have the world by its tail." Until he would discover, like his father, that he might not.

The country had never been more divided. The 1960s brought divisive attention to the changing dynamics of American life. It was culturally explosive, from the unraveling of Vietnam to the bloodied assassinations across America. Most parents were doing their best to shield their children from the disorder. It was no different for TJ and JR.

Father and son had not freely spoken about any aspect of America's wars. The topic seemed almost off limits. Since the Vietnam draft was in the wings, though, it was just a matter of time for the discussion to be had. Every day JR would walk by his father's desk and see the coveted plaque on his desk.

JR pressed him one day. "Dad, what was it like over there?" TJ paused before replying, "It was so long ago, it's hard to remember." JR smartly responded, "Did you think it was your duty?" TJ responded, "Yes," then with another brief pause, " ...As it might be yours someday."

They had begun the conversation in the subject matter of war. The two had harmony between the shared values of courage, respect, and public service. Nonetheless, their faith journey conjured up uncertainties in the arena of war. JR was prepared to take up the cause as his father had done for the good of country. However, the circumstances and times were different for the young man. The longer the American-Vietnam conflict played out, the more doubts surfaced for him and the nation at large.

One day TJ said to his son, "Why do you want to know so much about my time in Japan?" JR surprised him by saying, "This may sound crass ..." He continued, "But, who else will ever want to know? I may share a similar fate someday!" TJ looked stunned. JR was beside him ungluing some sticky pages of TJ's Pacific Rim book. TJ took the occasion to speak of the Marine discipline and honor code of "semper fidelis," though he never got personal.

Once, JR pushed the discussion further with, "Did you kill anyone?" TJ responded, "That's enough for now."

Eventually, JR decided to follow the tradition of his father. Ever unpopular to the end, he enlisted. He chose the Marines. At the time, the president was making an exasperated push into Cambodia for a finale. For all who served, it was an attempt to end something that would not die. The U.S. was never more divided with its politics as well as with its citizens.

JR prepared himself. He added *AMDG* to the same Marine creed his father took. One day, TJ saw his deployment papers. TJ responded, "What does this *AMDG* mean?"

JR was somewhat surprised. As good a Catholic his father was, he had no idea about the Jesuit culture. JR replied, "It means 'all for the honor and glory of God.'"

"Really," said his father. "Hmm, I never knew." He paused. "It would have come in handy for me in my day."

JR grabbed onto another opportunity for dialogue. "What do you mean, Dad?"

"Well," he said, "I was going off as you are now ..." He abruptly stopped and said, "I never understood how difficult it would be."

JR curiously followed, "What was so difficult?"

"Well," he said, "it was more ... the hardest thing."

Perplexed, JR gently pressed on. "What was the hardest thing, Dad?"

TJ looked up and stared as if transfixed in a trance. His last words stood adrift, as if he was absent from his mind in the faraway ground he occupied. JR had never seen him like this. Moisture started to yield in the older man's eyes.

TJ spoke. "I serve my country and I serve God. My duty was to my country and to my faith." He sighed and continued, "I was in command of troops. We executed successfully every mission placed in front of us. I helped build the first church in Kyushu. It burned down and then faith saw it rise again." JR sat and allowed a prolonged silence before his father went on. "I wrote letters and spent months in the ravages of sea trying to get home."

JR said gently, "I see, that is the hardest thing."

"No," the other countered abruptly. His gaze and attention drifted back to his son. "The hardest thing was when I returned home. After stepping onto the tarmac, no one was there to greet me."

Now with a tear in his own eye JR spontaneously blurted, "If I was alive, Dad, I would have been there to greet you."

XIX

JR's medical education and training provided him a unique position in the Marines. During school, he had developed a keen interest in the biomedical aspect of prosthetic engineering. It would serve great use in the field. Because of his knowledge of traumatic amputation, he was commissioned in scale. Like his father, enlistment gave him options and rank. At the time, he traveled with his college roommate, Tom, who enlisted as well, though more to the intent of avoiding the draft. They were to become commissioned field grade officers with the rank of major. It was above the company grade officer TJ had been given. It reflected the skills required in the collaborative effort within a special medical unit team.

In the recent past, Mobile Army Surgical Hospitals, called MASH in the vernacular, had been utilized in conflicts. Yet, limb salvage techniques, infection control, and sterility practices were still archaic at best. The U.S. military faced a new dilemma. Wounded soldiers in World War II accounted for five percent of amputations, whereas Vietnam climbed to twenty—in great part due to the land mines and close-range traps laid in guerilla warfare. A new model was necessary.

JR and Tom were commissioned to implement the Medical Unit Self-contained Transportable, a.k.a. MUST. This unique field hospital unit integrated comprehensive expandable self-containers for the purposes of surgery, radiography, and pharmaceutical distribution. For medical field management, it also included the first inflatable shelter ward for twenty or more. All was transported by helicopter in a drop-box container for ground assembly.

It was the next generation of immediate post-operative care. It was where the hospital came to the soldier patient. It was radical for the times. Given the two majors' expertise and command, they were also the chosen leaders in the implementation. The training would commence immediately. A particular Marine station in the West was the designated training site. California was to be revisited for a crossover by a new son. The only difference from his father's experience was that he had only one week to master the task. JR and Tom packed up. Hugs and well wishes were in order. They boarded a B-29 and flew out the following day.

Camp Pendleton was a whelping box for training. The new base was located near San Diego along the oceanside. A dozen prescribed crew teams were present. While in flight, JR and Tommy received and reviewed the officer manuals. On arrival, the team was assembled and readied. Once gathered, it was announced by Major Tom: "Our goal within the week will be to master the complete setup and operational use of the MUST units." Major JR followed, "At the end of the week, we will be timed for one hour operational from helicopter drop." They looked at each other for reassurance. Their leadership and skills would be tested from the start. It was ambitious, but not unattainable.

The majors reviewed the recruits. Both were surprised by the diversity and skill sets present. Without exception, the majors would place the demands on them as they would themselves. JR instructed the constructors to go ahead and begin. It harkened similar to his father's command in Sasebo.

A recruit caught JR's eye unexpectedly. He observed her unabashed tenacity to carry her weight, whatever the task. She quietly took the lead in expanding a transportable unit. Then she hand-sewed a cloth patch to the container tarp to seal oxygen lines into a surgical bay. As she finished, JR went to retrieve the extra fallen thread on the floor. Inadvertently, she turned to do the same. They gently bumped heads. She stepped back, beamed a bright smile, and said, "Hi, I'm Kami." The major was somewhat stunned by her bold response. It was atypical for a recruit to address an officer in such a way. Somehow, yet, he was smitten by her authentic manner and luminous presence. Uncharacteristically, he followed, "I'm JR." He continued, "Looks like we have the same aim." She replied, "Sure does."

The week went fast. The team mastered the setups and practiced the flow of simulated triage and recovery. Only one snafu occurred in the delivery of one hanging unit off the helicopter. Major Tom directed the drops inside the bay of the aircraft. Suddenly, a gust of wind coincided with the hovering drop on the knoll. In an instant, the major lost his grip on the cable release as the transport tipped to the side. The major tumbled from the bay onto the box fifteen feet below. A shriek of pain and a curse followed. "Damn! My leg!"

Sure enough, Tom had landed on the outside of his ankle. He was helped off the container. His ankle was ballooning as he reached down to place pressure on it. He abruptly said, "Man, this is bad. You got to get me to the hospital." JR begrudgingly smiled and followed, "No need. We got one here."

Tom was ushered into the set-up triage care unit. He was administered an instant cold pack, pain medication, and bandage wrap. Next, the latest equipment was employed to help determine the course of action. The MUST had the first portable fluoroscopy unit. Fluoroscopy was a new x-ray imaging technique that obtained real moving positions of the internal structures. It could diagnose and allow treatment at the same time. Manipulation of the segment back into place could be performed.

Tom was awake to see JR skillfully align and guide the distal fibula back into alignment. The major exclaimed, "That is so cool!" Utilizing new Gore-Tex lining and fiberglass casting, Major Tom was transferred to the recovery pod. He was then fit and trained with crutches by the physical therapist. He ambulated out of the unit in forty-five minutes. With that, the major became the first successfully treated patient in the MUST.

Major Tom still had one problem, however. He could no longer perform the rigors of field function in the duties of his ensuing deployment. So, he was ordered to stay in California. Like TJ and Art, JR had to part with his comrade and friend. "Looks like I'll need to cover this end of the fight!" said Tom. JR stated, "Yeah. Thanks for doubling my workload." They chuckled together. Tom bade farewell. "Hope it won't be long soon. It looks like Nixon is trying to broker a peace agreement. Good luck!" JR smiled and saluted. As he walked away, Tom uttered, "Oh! Keep your eye on that PT! She's my favorite of the bunch." JR was a bit confused. He had no idea who he was talking about.

As with most soldiers, the realization of leaving one's homeland prompted a pause for reflection in JR. He began his morning at the base chapel with early Mass. He always relied on his strong faith, especially when it was tested. It was a long flight to Hanoi, and he had never traveled outside the country.

The seventy-five hundred miles from Los Angeles would far eclipse his father's journey of sixty-five hundred from Milwaukee.

At Mass, he witnessed a somber crew in deep contemplation. By now, the newspapers published the war's unfolding unpopularity as casualties and protests mounted. Despite this, the medical team's service meant all the more to the cause.

After Mass, the presiding priest stated he would remain for reconciliation. JR stayed in the pew for a moment in reflection and prayer. In all his preparations, it had been awhile since his last confession. He prepared earnestly now, knowing that this would very likely be his last opportunity. He spent confessional time reviewing his life's conciliations to this point. He thought himself a defender of the weak and underserved, but now focused on his own omissions, significance, and sense of humility. In his desire to make himself the go-to person and self-effacing competitor, he had come to feel trapped in his own self, his own truths and his own doing.

The priest was consoling. The absolution left him in a quiet presence. Before JR raised himself from the confessional kneeler, the priest spoke these words: "My son, remember, he who grows in holiness, always has a strong sense of failure."

The young major went back to his pew and knelt to reflect and pray. A despondent sense of aloneness and vulnerability came over him. He breathed deep, allowing an opening for the Spirit to flow. He started to recollect his writings in high school with the designation *AMDG* under his name. With a renewed sense of meekness, he prayed for the graces to let go and place God's honor and glory above his own name in the future.

It was a lonely time in every soldier's chapter. Yet, he knew he was not alone, remembering his father and many more doing the same. JR began to realize the trust walk between faith and the bond of duty as an American. He committed to opening a page to a low regard for himself and trusting in a better way going forward.

He stood to genuflect and leave the chapel when he noticed in his periphery the female recruit he had met the first day of training. Her eyes were closed as she sat tall in the pew. He paused, struck by the peaceful presence on her face—almost as if she was contemplating a calming awareness no one else could perceive.

XX

The flight took off on time. It was a long flight. They would break for fueling in the Marshall Islands. Because of the international dateline, the time skipped forward to the next day. They were glad to disembark and stretch their legs during the layover.

During World War II, these islands were Japanese territories to be strategically invaded. They served as a premier launching site for the bombers to reach Tokyo. Little had TJ known that thirty years later, they would have been repurposed from a long-range bombing station to become JR's last stop before Southeast Asia.

As they flew over to land, one could not help but notice an aerial view of eerie keyhole-shaped mounds of earth. Upon arrival, the crew was given an extended break to reset their biological clocks. The islands had a beautiful chain of beach stretches to enjoy. They were on leave until the break of dawn. They departed the aircraft and were ordered to gather on the tarmac. One of the crewmembers asked the major what those mound figures meant. When the major shrugged his shoulders, Kami spoke up.

"I think they are called the holy grounds of the ancients here. Better known as Kofun." She continued, "They were constructed in the favor of class and principle. The noblest are found within the keyhole. They are known for their selfless contribution to society. The shapes represent the bending of the earth's irrigation so as to facilitate rice and crops for sustenance. The mounds display the engineering prowess of those times and are honored as such."

One of the men jumped in stating, "I bet we can dig one up and find buried treasure!"

Kami immediately replied, "These are a people of ancient temples and shrines. It is a sacred site."

The major took voice. "Okay guys, we are here on a break, not an excavation." They all dispersed. He turned to Kami and asked, "So, do you also know how long they have been here?"

"Yes, Major, since the fourth century."

"How do you know all this?"

"You might say I have ancestry here."

As dawn broke, JR walked along the ocean shoreline. He wished he could stretch up into the sky far enough to see the coastline of California. At Camp Pendleton, he had had only an afternoon to swim out into the surf waves. He took advantage of a dip now. He enjoyed the blissful buoy of the salt water, unlike what he experienced on Lake Michigan. He sat with his face to the first light of day. In the soft break of the waves, he drifted back.

He remembered the special day when his father bought a boat. He was asked to help wax and shine it up for its inaugural launch. TJ alone would commandeer it. He steered it like a PT-109 through the smooth lake waters. He and Helen would take out the family and make a day of it. Sandwiches, sodas, and the occasional beer would burst up from the ice chest. TJ got a kick out of swinging the water skiers as far out in front of the boat as possible, as if unable to turn around back to see. When anchored, he would move to the bow of the boat and practice a rehearsal dive off the side. Then he would follow with a signature belly flop into the water. Everyone laughed, exclaiming that the waves he created were larger than any skier's wake. It was in those carefree timeless moments where freedom, peace, and family stood still. The major closed his eyes, hoping this vision would go on forever. Such was his and TJ's love for the water. It was their ultimate solace.

The morning sun lightened his lids. He opened his eyes to the luminous low-lying cumulus clouds of purple and pink hues. It was then he could hear the rhythmical sounds of slaps and kicks off the reef. It was a graceful swimmer greeting the day.

XXI

They touched down in Saigon. Their connection to the base was through an officer named Sutibu. He was hard to miss outside customs. He held a sign reading *MOORENES!* and seemed genuinely excited to see them. He exclaimed in English, "We have been expecting you! You will be transported to the base hospital." He continued, "I have good news! Come outside with me?" JR cautiously nodded to his crew. He was somewhat apprehensive, as this was not the reception he expected. As they exited the terminal, they felt the sweltering heat and humidity. It hit them like a ton of bricks.

The city was wildly ecstatic, with beeping horns and jumping people in the streets. The major and crew looked around, wondering how a war-torn city could be so festive. Then they saw signs and Vietnamese flags waving joyfully. A young Vietnamese ran up to JR and embraced him with a hug. He cried without restraint, "The war is over!!"

JR and TJ shared at least one thing in common in their experience overseas. They were present when the wars had ended. JR reached to catch an air-blown newspaper in his path. The Saigon newspaper headline said it all: "U.S. Congress passes Case-Church Amendment to end the war." He folded it and shoved it in his pocket for later digestion.

To the major, it seemed to end before it even started for him. The crew was amazed at the craze of the exuberance. The once torn North and South were now celebrating together in dance with raised flags. It was like an overdue reunion. Sutibu waved his hand and gathered the Americans around him. He cleared his throat to speak. "This is the good news. Now, come with me in the vans for the next news." The major and crew obliged. They cruised through the ravaged streets of Saigon. The dimples of rounds on buildings could be seen all around. The only areas unscathed were the fruit and vegetable stands.

They stopped abruptly to allow some locals to carry a statue of Ho Chi Ming across a street. Finally, they turned into the entrance gates of a hospital. Some official documents were submitted to the guards. The gate was raised as they proceeded to the entrance. Sutibu opened the door and ushered all out. He conveyed, "I will make sure all your gear and supplies arrive here safely. This is where you will stay and perform your work. Welcome to Saigon Hospital." He paused. "Now maybe Ho Chi Ming City Hospital."

The crew all looked at the major. It was confusing. It seemed like a whole new assignment. JR ordered them to wait while he stepped into the main corridor. A distinctive white-coated woman greeted him in English, "Thank you for coming." She continued, "My name is Captain Reiko. I am a doctor physiatrist. This is the relocated mission base." She went on, "With the end of war, North Vietnam has now taken over South Vietnam. Your expertise from America will serve here. The fieldwork is no longer needed. All the conflict casualties are here. Please, let me take you and your team around." The major excused himself and waved his team into the hospital. As they gathered he spoke up with assurance: "Welcome to command center."

Dr. Reiko ushered them around an organized medical complex. It was divided into two divisions, the American ward on the first floor and South Vietnamese on the second to tenth floors. The tenth was the top. They were subcategorized into emergency intensive, orthopedic, neurological, infectious disease, internal, pediatric, and post-operative care and rehabilitation. The major asked, "How many bed injured do you have?" She stated, "Currently?" She paused. "Seventy-five American and a thousand South Vietnamese." A gasp came from the crew, "That's huge!" Dr. Reiko followed, "Now you see why you are here. I hope this is not the bad news." Just then, Sutibu returned to the group and spoke, "The luggage and supplies have arrived." Dr. Reiko interrupted, "It will be placed in the dormitories behind the hospital. We begin tomorrow on the patient care." She left them and Sutibu resumed with, "Follow me."

The dorm rooms were sectioned in concrete blocks. They had the feeling of an old prison. JR loosened his collar and lay back on the cot. It was not what he expected, none of it. As he welcomed the long post-flight sleep, he reached into his pocket and retrieved the folded news from earlier. He stretched it out and read the front page. It read, *Unanimous vote in Congress to end America's role in Southeast Asia and bring the troops home.* He then scanned down to the Defense Casualty Analysis Report in small print at the bottom of the page. It continued, *Current 58,000 U.S. military casualties.* It highlighted a further statistic. *1 in 10 American personnel have been killed or wounded, including 1 out of every 4 Marines.* He paused for a sigh.

Thus far, the toll on the war among the Vietnamese was just beginning to trickle in. According to U.S. government figures, an estimated two million Vietnamese civilians had been killed and five million injured. The hospital census started to make sense. JR did not know what to expect starting the next morning. Nonetheless, he knew his mission and crew were ready to carry on. That evening, he wrote to his parents. Like his father, he was at the beginning of his own repatriation phase. Before he turned the light off, he took a last glance at the back article of the newspaper he had placed down. It read, *Nixon de-escalation of war now shifts to deepening probe into Watergate.*

The casualties were much worse than imagined. The war had showed no forgiveness to either side. Sutibu escorted the major and staff medical crew to the floor housing the Americans. As the wing doors opened, JR could see neatly organized rows with light netting around each of the beds. With the quarters so tight, airborne diseases as well as malaria were free to reign. Dr. Reiko proceeded into the room and said, "I am glad you are starting work." She continued, "This side is orthopedic cases and the other side neurologic."

As they walked among the beds, the GIs perked with lifted spirits. The range of grievances was apparent, from defoliant chemical exposure to head injuries. They received the procedural care follow-up with sterile precautions. Next implemented were casted limb traction devices from trauma. Most were restless. The predominant belief revolved around soon being granted leave for home.

One heavily bandaged soldier glared at the major with a cigarette dangling from his mouth. The major spoke up to the soldier. "We are here to help. I know it has been bad out there." The soldier released a long stream of smoke and replied, "Mayhem, sir." He continued, "One side in disarray with the other. Wild West command and firing at will. Like trapped mice, no effective backup and no way out." Another soldier chimed in, "Anything that moved we shot at. Little knowing what was there and where it was coming from." He winced. "I was shot at multiple times retrieving one of our men." The major told him, "You will be honored for that!" The man replied, "I don't know, sir. Most didn't make it. I am not sure what honor holds with me as a savior." JR sighed and saluted. Nothing more could be said. Still another soldier next to him added, "The only thing good about this situation are the cigarettes. Otherwise, this is a god-forsaken hellhole."

Dr. Reiko finished the rounds on the American floors. She then took them to the Vietnamese floors. She turned to them and said frankly, "This is where you are needed." As they opened up the door, a stench filled the air.

It became a sight that none could forget. It was not just the moaning and lack of provisions. It was the pain and shock that colored the Vietnamese' faces. The third floor hit the major the hardest. He witnessed a sight that would forever be embedded in his psyche. Rows of children stretched the far length and width of the floor. An abyss of estranged innocence with mangled fractures and missing limbs.

In the end, the MUST units were late in field conflict implementation. JR could see the war had been particularly harsh on the little ones. They reflected the cruelty of engagement. The Vietnamese were expert in luring the Americans into the jungles and villages for ambush. Delicately placed and covered land mines were skillfully intentional. However, children were not privy to the selected locations. Families were displaced from village to village, only to encounter the untapped traps. An intricate underground web system had been woven for surprise attack. Most would never know if the mines were placed from above or below. For the children, discovery was only in the detonation process, triggered by a misplaced hop or step during their chores or the games they played. The lure of machete pathways could not distinguish an age for suffering.

JR walked down the floor of rowed children. Their big eyes looked back at him wondering if another nightmare walked through or possibly a redeemer of hope. He scanned their faces as they stooped in their places to just stare at him. It was like looking down a long boundary line in a football field. The major put down his pack. He turned to Dr. Reiko and spoke. "We are ready to begin."

His mission unveiled itself. It wasn't long before he subdivided his crew for the acutely injured to more chronically ill in preparation for release. The major personally tackled the below-knee amputations, as they could be fitted with some form of a prosthetic. He had to be creative and ingenious with what he had. He used the fiberglass tape with sterile cloth bandaging and socks. The materials could be sewn up for limb protection during load bearing. He had PVC forms from the MUST units and bamboo from the locals to fabricate pylons. This could be used to connect sockets to the ground. Finally, he utilized tires from military vehicles. These could be cut to serve as a surface to rock over in walking. Put it all together, and he created an ambulatory postoperative prosthesis. The only problem was that he needed a good seamstress. "Yes," he surmised, "Kami!"

A first child volunteered. The rest, intrigued, scurried in fashion to surround JR and Kami. They wooed as they observed how a foreign substance could harden and fix to a perceived plastic pipe and tire. The material that Kami would hand-sew was wrapped around the limb, marked, and outlined. It would serve to encapsulate the anatomy that would become a socket liner for the wrap. The major would dip the fiberglass rolls into water and layer the material strips of varying thickness around, to cushion and protect the flesh. It would brace around the PVC pylon. The support would be cut and adjusted to even lengths matching the child's corresponding sound limb. Finally, the tire treading was placed on the end for grip and traction.

In great anticipation, the first child cautiously stood. The children wooed again and clapped. Kami turned to JR and asked, "How did you come up with this?" The major replied, "It just came to me." The child peered down the hall and spoke something in Vietnamese as if asking for permission. JR shrugged his shoulders and looked at Kami. Kami balanced the boy to walk with a reassuring hand and voice. The boy let go. He ran reaching high with his hands in the air. All the children cheered.

Dr. Reiko brought in food consisting of curried rice, water, and tea. She sighed as she sat with them.

She spoke with a concerning voice, "The Americans call them 'scatterable.' We call them the 'eternal sentinels.'" Somewhat confused, JR questioned her. "What are you referring to?" She continued, "The worst man-made disaster of the century, even more evil than the atomic bomb." They perked up for a further explanation. She spoke wearily, "In the field, we saw them scattered in flight from the helicopters. They fluttered to the ground like butterflies, gently landing. The children would run up to them as if they believed to be showered with toys from the sky. Then they would explode once discovered." She went on, "When planted in the field, children would come running and trip a thin wire connected to the explosive. The parents would bring them to us in shock for help. Very few would survive. We could not stop the bleeding from the imbedded shrapnel." She paused. "Why is it that the malevolence of the decision makers causes the most innocent to suffer?" A long silence penetrated the room. The major then spoke, "Well, it is now over." Dr. Reiko cleared her voice. "Not for the future of these little ones." She continued, "Do you know why we call the traps the 'eternal sentinels'?" The major nodded, respectfully silent. She went on, "It is because they never sleep. Always ready for attack. In an instant, they are ready to take and deny life. This is what we face." She then stood, "I must excuse myself. I must attend to the others." She bowed and walked away to another floor.

A dozen below-knee amputee children were fit on day one. It was just the beginning. The major made rounds every day. His team administered triage, cleaned infections, changed bandages, and mobilized patients. He was happy to see them make the transition and practice their disciplines. He long remembered a most troubling sight from one afternoon when he came down a stairwell to the floor containing the children. He entered from the back end of the floor this time. A young girl raised her arm in a wave at him with bandages fluttering all around. As he waved back, he took further notice to see indeed her forearm waving without a hand. Anguish came over him. He returned to where Kami was sewing the liners for limbs. He sat down and placed his hand on his forehead as if unloading a weight. He then felt the head of Kami rest upon his shoulder. She smiled as they rested for the moment.

A month passed as the major and crew worked together to provide the necessary care and renew physical function to the disabled. JR encouraged his team to treat all and not diminish fair treatment to the injured rivalry present. After all, the war was over and rebuilding was at hand. Again and again he again found solace in Kami. Her contagious gentle smile and unfaltering passion to help all suffering held no bounds. Her reassuring glances helped him endure the long days and reaffirmed the benevolence and compassion he found inside himself.

One day, JR noticed a note slipped under his door in the morning. He opened it. *Meet me at the front gate at 9:00 a.m.*, signed by Dr. Reiko. JR dressed and proceeded to the gate. A car pulled up and he was asked to get in. He looked inside and saw Dr. Reiko and a finely dressed woman.

They sped off as introductions were made. Dr. Reiko began. "Major, please meet Official Minister Ayako from Japan. She is the special goodwill ambassador for human rights. Her organization is the Nippon Foundation. Their interest is in humanitarian work for our people. I told her that you and your medical team have special services in rehabilitation."

"Konnichiwa! *Genki desu ka?*" the minister spoke.

"Konnichiwa!" the major replied, somewhat surprised by the Japanese language. He continued, *"Eigo?"*

"Yes," the ambassador said.

They turned a corner and got out at a storefront restaurant. Not sure what all this was about, JR looked forward to a good meal at least. They sat at a table. The minister began, "We have an interest we share." She went on. "In our philanthropic work, we have provided mobile clinics throughout these areas. I know you have brought some as well. But our interest now is in the next step." Intrigued by her thoughts, JR leaned in. She continued, "Our team needs to be educated in the provision of state-of-the-art prosthetics. If you are interested, we would like you to come to Japan and help us set up this coalition to assist in our efforts and aid our neighbors here who have suffered much."

The major was fascinated. However, he spoke with his sense of duty. "I do have my assignment here and lead for my crew."

She followed, "I am aware of that. They are in good hands here. They can stay or return stateside in accordance with the new peace withdrawal agreement." She went on, "I would appreciate your consideration. I can be in touch with your superiors to allow this to happen."

A tad flummoxed, the major replied, "Well, it is my hope to assist in any way I can."

"Arigato, *gozaimasu!*" exclaimed the minister in Japanese.

Dr. Reiko cracked a smile. "So," she put in, "I have ordered the best dishes in Saigon for the occasion."

As the food arrived, JR's eyes widened. He had never seen so many dry roasted insects and gummy-type eels infused into an omelet. JR responded, "Is this the specialty?" Dr. Reiko spoke, "It is the unique delicacy of the area." She raised her glass and exclaimed, "Kanpai!" Cautiously, he raised his glass of water and proceeded to test the specialty.

On the way back, gratitude was exchanged. Dr. Reiko and the major exited the car. As they walked through the gate, the major informed the doctor, "I will need to tell my crew." He continued, "They will need to be relieved to the next command, to stay or be provided passage home." "I will give them those options," Dr. Reiko followed. "Know that they are most welcome here." They walked to the front doors of the hospital. Before they departed to begin the day's work, JR spoke up without thought to his words. "When we have hope for ourselves, we have hope for humanity."

Dr. Reiko gave him a contented smile. Without hesitation, she leaned over and kissed him on the cheek.

JR continued treating the wounded that morning, as did his team. He continually taught and assisted his crew, as to support and refine techniques of the work. He soon announced he would speak to them at a break around noon. He exited to the stairwell for a moment to collect his thoughts. It seemed uncharacteristic to contemplate his command leave, much less an unscheduled venture into an unknown. But then again nothing was of the ordinary since he had arrived. He knew he would be understood if he spoke from the heart. He gathered his crew together. They circled around the major like committed followers.

He began, "You all know that this has been a trust walk since we arrived. Nothing has been as we predicted. But such are the times we live in. If anything, we will be remembered for what we are doing and how much we affect these lives. As you know and as you see all around, very little security is offered in the world we live. But, that is not why we are here. If we have learned anything since our arrival, it is to embrace the impossible in what we do, as we have liberated hope where there was none. In my command, you have been the most excellent comrades. All worthy of stepping into my shoes at a moment's notice. For that I am truly encouraged and grateful."

He paused to glance around to see them within the enclosure of his presence. He continued, "Yet, a new sun is rising. Another horizon waits. It is not my desire, but the desire of a greater purpose that bids me away. I have been asked to join an alliance that will take me to Japan. It is for a cause that will affect our consequences of what we do here and at home. You are free to stay and continue the work or carry back home the distinguished duty you have faithfully performed. Command has designated Captain Dr. Reiko to your further needs and duties. Good day and good luck, my comrades." He saluted them in unison as they saluted back. To the last recruit, he asked if he knew all were present. He replied, "Yes, sir, all but Officer Kami."

He returned to his quarters. He heard a knock at the door. He opened to it. "Official business from the consulate," proclaimed a courier. He handed JR a large envelope and promptly excused himself. The major opened it. It had an air ticket with official leave documents from the U.S. embassy. Also, a note from Minister Ayako was found inside. It read:

> *Thank you. We have great hope in our mission and convictions. I, too, was once apprehensive in a difficult time. I sought hope in rebuilding my life when all I had left was courage. I trust you will find the same. My best, Ayako.*

JR sat for a moment. He thought of his father. He remembered him talking about the rebuilding of Japan. Now, a similar mission of hope and repatriation spoke to him.

XXII

JR took a long walk through the streets of Saigon that afternoon. He stumbled upon a street vendor who gave him a bowl of dry squid porridge and spring rolls. He was just getting used to the food. He strolled through Tao Dan Park where protests once rang next to the manicured gardens at the foot of a Buddhist temple. He watched as the local children played games. He imagined the first amputee child he had treated doing the same.

Suddenly, something astonished him back to reality. The children started to vanish. Not even foot scampering to be heard. Perplexed, he wandered closer to the area. As he looked over the hedge where they had been romping around moments ago, nothing was seen. He mumbled to himself, "What the heck happened to them?" As he stepped further onto the grassy knoll, a pop from below startled him. He was surprised and shaken when a square grassy cover popped from the ground with two small hands pushing it up. The child smirked and laughed in delight. Suddenly, a second popped up behind him. It soon became clear to JR it was a playground network of tunnels. It was a reality that brought him back to the stark contrasts that existed between his home and this place.

He made his way over to a Gothic stone building. It stretched skyward over the indigenous dipterocarp trees. It was a basilica. In the front stood a statue of Mother Mary, with arms open as an invitation into the sanctuary of Notre Dame. He had hardly expected to find such magnificence here. When the Communists took the city, they left the square at peace. Miraculously, the site remained unscathed. It seemed that the only thing that changed was the name of Saigon to Ho Chi Minh City. It was if Mary represented a form of North-South reunification. He took the symbolism as encouragement for him to make his way to the church.

A plaque in the front stated it was once the site of a Vietnamese pagoda. The first invaders of French conquest left their mark in its reconstruction as a Catholic cathedral. He sat in the back admiring the Romanesque features, stained glass, and painted nave. He could see Mass going on in the front so he sat closer to observe and participate. At Communion, he stood to receive the Eucharist. As he moved behind the recipient ahead, he recognized the familiar profile.

It was Kami. As he received and returned to his pew, he reached forward to place his hand on her shoulder before she turned to kneel. He sensed that familiar smile, yet was unable to see in passing by to take his place.

After Mass, he sat on the basilica steps outside. She exited as well and sat at his side. He started, "I am not sure you know, but I am leaving on assignment tomorrow morning."

"I have heard," she answered.

Surprised for a second, he went on, "It seems to be my fate to answer the need that is calling me."

She gently replied, "It is good that you are aware of this." She continued, "I am sure you have weighed this carefully and sought in your heart for what is best."

"Yes," he said, weighing. "Although, I believe I have met my match in my aim to seek that which is best."

She smiled. "I know you will awaken to the greatest good inside yourself."

He awkwardly continued, "I hesitate to leave. You have become a meaningful part of my journey. It is hard to explain. Yet, in some way, I feel I must go undeterred."

She tenderly reassured him. "I see this match in aim as well. I can only hope for that best we speak of." Kami beamed into his eyes. It was a look he was certain of. She placed her hand on his knee. "Whether we go or stay, whether we wait and see, it makes no difference. A match is a match. I am here. You are here. I will be there. You will be there. I will be. You will be." They held hands, hesitating to stand, not to lose the attentive gaze on each other.

Without warning, a man stumbled down the basilica steps and landed on the street. He cried out in pain, holding his head. JR and Kami, suddenly startled, jumped up. The priest appeared questioning, "What happened here?" Kami looked down to see the man's scalp bleeding, leaving a trail down his face. She raced down to inspect his head and assess the gash. She looked up to the priest. "Do you have a bandage or cloth? Clean water?" The priest replied, "Everything is put away inside! Wait! We have holy water in the baptistery."

Without hesitation, she did something surely miraculous and perhaps just shy of blasphemous. She looked about with a keen eye and zeroed in on the priest. She went up and placed her hands around the back of his neck. She swiftly grabbed hold of the cloth scapula lying on his shoulders and she looped it over his head. She then bolted to the baptismal fountain. She carefully layered the cloth into the water and squeezed gently to let it drain. She hustled back through the doors of the church. She found the man sitting now with his hands over his blood-smeared face. She cradled his head with the holy vestment. She began to wrap it in a serpentine fashion, anchoring it under his chin. The bleeding stopped.

All the while JR and the priest looked on with amazement. Kami finally spoke. "I'll take him to the hospital. More can be done for him there." With that, she looped the man's arm over her shoulder and walked with him away. The priest turned to JR and said, "To think, I give absolution with that vestment." He paused to continue, "She knew how to heal with it."

JR's flight was at 9:00 a.m. He got up early, packed his things, and thought an early morning run would do him good. He ran around the park, faster in his jog than usual. He was now acutely aware of the little Vietnamese "gophers" that popped up in surprise. The sun was rising. He made his turn around the basilica. He jogged in place for a moment in front of the statuary of Our Lady's opened arms. He stopped to wipe the sweat from his brow.

The priest had already opened the great wooden gated doors to the congregation for morning Mass. He glanced over and recognized the major. "You coming in for Mass?" he sounded.

JR replied, "Sorry, Father, have to catch a flight."

"Where is your brave friend?"

"Oh," JR said, "I'm on my own."

The priest walked down the steps towards him as if to deliver one last departing word. "I am sorry, my son, you seemed to know her well." JR appeared awkward to answer. The priest continued, "Do you know some Scripture?"

JR, somewhat surprised, sputtered, "Well, yes, at least some, Father."

The priest went on, "Do you know Matthew 13?"

Aback, the major replied, "I'm not entirely sure."

The priest reached into his pocket and presented a small Bible. He reached for JR's arm and placed it in his hand. The priest spoke, "Read Matthew 13 verses 46 to 48 sometime." He followed, "You have found something quite rare." He traced the sign of the cross on JR's head and blessed him for a safe way. JR thanked him and proceeded to leave. As he walked back by the statue of Mary, he looked up and paused quietly. He stood still to ponder the mystery of women in faith. A car then screeched up. Out popped the minister with, "I have your bags. All is in order. We have to get to the airport."

It was a similar flight as the one from the Marshall Islands to Saigon. After takeoff, Ayako questioned the distracted major from his stare out the window. "Have you forgotten something?" she asked. The major sighed and unconvincingly shook his head. She attentively began a new conversation. "In this new position, may I call you JR?" The major pushed back into his seat from his trance. "Yes," he replied, "and may I call you Ayako?" She responded, "Hai!" They both smiled.

Once at altitude, JR turned to her. "So," he spoke. "Why have you brought me with you?" She paused briefly before replying. "Dr. Reiko spoke highly of your new methods and skills during my visit. You have the representative qualities we are looking for." JR looked somewhat puzzled. "Let me explain. Recently, the World Medical Association has approved our Declaration of Tokyo. It is the newly adopted guideline for practicing medicine in the service of our fellow man. It describes the doctor's role as to preserve and restore physical and mental health without discriminating between individuals." She continued, "It sanctions the practice of torture, cruelty, or degradation through medical knowledge and treatments contrary to the humanity of patients."

JR nodded his head in understanding and agreement. He then spoke up about his father. "During World War II, my father was in command of a prison built by the captured. It was a difficult time just after surrender. He was compassionate and refocused their energy into the construction of a church. He stayed to participate in the repatriation phase."

Ayako curiously responded, "Where was he stationed?" JR stated, "He was in the Kyushu prefecture." She replied, "I am from that area," then added, "What city was he in?" JR responded, "I believe he said Sasebo." "Oh yes," she responded. "It is near my home in Kokura."

Ayako closed her eyes and drifted to sleep. JR could not sleep, instead drifting back to his last moments with Kami on the church steps. Since the beginning of the flight, JR had felt a nagging rectangular lump in his front pocket. Eventually he carefully arched back into his seat to pull it out. He recognized it as the Bible from the priest. He recalled the New Testament passage the priest had mentioned. The plane banked around Tokyo Bay, framing Mount Fuji through the window during the final descent. Before JR put his seatbelt back on, he opened the book and paged to Matthew 13:46-47. It read:

> *Once again, the kingdom of heaven is like a merchant in search of fine pearls; on finding one pearl of great value, he went and sold all he had and bought it."*

XXIII

Tokyo was now the third largest city in the world. The locals referred to it as Edo. Skyscrapers were wedged in between Shinto shrines and Buddhist temples. The metropolis intricately displayed the balance and precision of both the traditional and the modern. As they flew over the middle of the city, JR got his first look at the imposing gates and castle-like structures.

He turned to Ayako. "What are those structures and large green spaces?" Ayako replied, "The great tori." She went on, "The gate represents the entrance to a sacred shrine. What you see is the Meiji. It represents reform, consolidation, and renewal of Japanese imperial rule." She continued, "Emperor Meiji began the modernization of Japan knowing we were behind the advancements of the Western world. The castle is Tokyo's imperial palace. It is the residence of the emperor and his family. Much of it was destroyed in the Allied air raids during the war. The grounds and palace have been restored now." JR expressed, "Meiji is an interesting and strange name for an emperor." Ayako responded, "*Meiji* means 'enlightened rule.' You must go there sometime."

JR said, "If part of the goal is for me to go, then I will oblige." Ayako replied, "Our goal is to combine modern advances with traditional values. You will see soon."

They landed at Haneda International Airport. Being built over waterfront land, it reflected a system of modernized efficiency. Once an army air base, it now shined with architectural glass shapes and complementary lined struts. It had been the entry showcase for the Olympics of 1964. A unique train network operated above their heads. Ayako pointed, "That will take us to the hotel downtown. She paused to continue, "It is the first commercial monorail in the world." She turned to him and said, "Welcome to Tokyo."

They arrived downtown at a traditional Japanese inn called a *ryokan*. It was across from Tokyo Tower. It was the tallest broadcasting center at the time. They were met by a stately man wearing wire-rimmed glasses and carrying a walking stick. Ayako introduced JR. "Dr. Isao, please meet Major JR." *Konnichiwa*s were jointly exchanged. Dr. Isao added, "The foundation welcomes you." He continued, "Please call me Isao," and then bowed.

They proceeded into the Japanese guesthouse. All removed their shoes in favor of the traditional slippers provided them. Seating was at a low table on tatami mats. The servants entered. They were geishas. One retreated into the corner plucking a stringed instrument. The atmosphere was relaxed and soothing. The three guests were brought tea. JR inquired, "What tea is this?" Isao replied, "Matcha." A dinner was presented of sashimi blue fin tuna, ginger, wasabi, and yakisoba. After dinner, a bottle of sake was opened and poured into small ceramic cups. A toast was proposed from Isao. "Here is to our work." He nodded and continued, "Share the pain, share the hope, and share the future. Kanpai!"

Then Isao elucidated his meaning to JR. "We are bringing to the world a new vision of medical care. Not just for those who have the means, but those who might not and perhaps never will.

We are creating a framework to bring about change in which all people support one another." He expounded, "Our projects include support for seriously ill children with disabilities, special adoption, child poverty, disaster recovery, and reconstruction. We intend to be the hub for social innovation in Japan and around the world. Our goal is to give all of humanity the chance to participate in creating the future." He paused and added, "I know bringing people together creates synergies. Our priority is solving problems on the ground, much like what you were doing in Saigon. That is our vision and that is why you are here."

JR sat back. He paused to think to himself, "How did this happen?" If only his father were here to ask. Would TJ see a transformed society that was once beaten to the ground rise? Had he ever thought this possible to occur? Precipitously, JR felt he had been prepared for this. With a deep certainty he sensed a universal good, honor, and glory in Isao's purpose.

JR spoke freely, "I am without words except a few from the heart. This is truly extraordinary and unprecedented. You place on the table a utopia of borderless collaboration. Call it a synergy of mutual bonds across all humanity. It is so different from what I have learned and understood, yet so much in alignment. Thank you."

"Excellent!" responded Isao. "We begin after your holiday."

JR had never stayed in a ryokan before. He was most intrigued by the natural springs known as the *onsen*. He decided to try it before retiring. He entered into the geothermal ready to soak. However, he did not understand the rules. The Japanese had a procedure. An elder gestured to him with motions to thoroughly shower and scrub down before entering. He did so, but then was stopped again. The elder implied that no clothing of any sort was allowed. Somewhat embarrassed in the buff, JR stepped down into the two feet of water, following the cues of the senior. There was no talk as all rested their heads back on a step. It was customary to project a loud sighing groan once settled, as to release the stress of life into the steamed air. In fact, it seemed more like a ritualistic practice of cleansing and purification. Nonetheless, he found it most comfortable, meditative, and relaxing. The elders concluded with a bow when done.

He retired to his room. New slippers awaited his feet at the doorway before he walked in. The space was simple in taste: futon, table, and chair separated by a sliding shoji panel. He noticed a fine calligraphy brush and paper. He sat and decided to write. He wrote a letter to his father and mother. He had much to tell about his journey.

He started the morning with his usual jog. He soon slowed to attend the fish markets. He observed the knife skills of the chefs. They prepared blades with ground precision against a flat stone. Oiled and watered, each wave of the knife cleanly sleeved the fishes' glistening flesh. Fresh octopus, snapper, squid, tuna, and roe were manicured in lotus shapes as if meant for displaying their plate for artistic consecration. The women would pinch fresh wasabi into miniature Fuji mounts along with squeezed rivers of dark soy and pads of ginger.

The sight was too much not to indulge. The Japanese gastronomic masters perfected portion sizes that would be consumed in full without a trace left afterward. The phrase "bust a gut" referred to a compliment and a way of consumption here. As JR walked from stall to stall, he could see the simplicity of life. Here, many lived directly behind the stalls as the youth observed and learned from the ways of the masters.

He continued his stroll to the wide spread of gardens. Never before had he seen such precision, detail, and care to the enveloping and sculpting of the life in earth and water. It was a dance of appreciation of one element with the other. Carp nestled under the trained cascading bonsai, seeking refuge from the arching sun. Lotus leaves floated weightless on the water as turtles poked curious foreheads above the surface. On occasion, a blooming lotus would be spotted. A caught water droplet could occasionally be caught resting still at the plant's base, delicately cupped without quiver. A crane would stand still. Its beak would pierce through the waveless waters, then it would retract its neck in a serpentine posture. Each component participated equally in the balanced Zen of this aquatic garden refuge.

He soon discovered a multiple-story pagoda. It towered to the sky with projecting wings inviting raptors to perch. He entered one and sat quietly in the back on a tatami. He contemplated the tremendous girth of the timber columns. Nowhere were these sizes seen except in the great heights of the mountains. What effort must have been spent by man and beast to get these to such destinations at the time of construction. A couple entered and sat before the Buddha in the central sanctuary, becoming as a painted image of meditation and contemplation before transcendence.

Tokyo Tower was an imposing structure that radiated the telecommunications in every direction. It symbolized the latest developments and happenings in the city. An elevator took JR to the top. He could view the great Tokyo Bay and the imposing features of the tallest mountain in Japan, Fuji. He wished he had the time to climb it, but that would have to wait.

The major traveled back to his ryokan through the narrow streets of Ginza. He slipped into a stand-up counter soba shop. He ordered only the specialties, with a large bowl of buckwheat noodles in broth to follow. He mimicked the locals in slurping the soba down, lifting the bowl to hug the face. Chopsticks were only used to guide the noodles' path. The frequent belch was freed as a compliment of good food and a sought-out, established statement of gratitude. Finally, a sip of sake satisfied the meal and completed the touch of the cuisine. It was time for a full day to end. The sun turned red as it lowered to the horizon.

XXIV

The new day came all too soon. The major rose at the tap on the door. Upon opening, he was met with a vibrant green powder, a ceramic hot water kettle, and a handle-less cup on a standing bamboo tray. He promptly took it inside. He mixed the green matcha and sipped leisurely. He showered while looking at a windowed view of the courtyard pond which was brimming with carp and colorful lotus. He dressed and walked to the front gate, refreshed for what the day would bring.

Ayako and Isao greeted him at the entrance. "Today, you will lecture to our staff and students on the innovations you have brought." With a mutual nod, the three taxied to Tokyo Medical University Hospital. Isao informed JR, "This is our major teaching hospital. It has over three thousand beds and a staff of one thousand. Our team includes all Allied health professionals and physicians. You will have their full attention."

They entered a tiered lecture hall. JR walked onto the main stage floor. He detected an incense waft that reminded him of the Mass he had attended at Notre Dame Basilica, where he had run into Kami. He turned his head to the right to discover the scent trailing from a temple shrine. As the hospital personnel gathered, seats filled throughout the amphitheater. JR stood at center stage at the ready to conduct his audience.

An amputee child on a wheeled plinth was brought to center stage. JR looked at and greeted him with great interest and compassion. This child would be his testimony. Materials, casting, and surgical supplies were placed on a table and rolled up onto the stage as well. A reflective mirror was lowered and angled to demonstrate the methods to be exhibited to the whole audience. The boy grinned and nodded to JR as if a trust already existed.

JR knew his work and presentation skills. He was well prepared. But, something now changed. His life up to this moment accumulated into a force more than his own doing. He did not have to remember where to stand or what to say.

Momentarily, he closed his eyes, then inhaled and exhaled the incense so familiar as it transcended to him at the podium. From that instant, his presentation captured the learners with the depth of his instructional expertise. He began with the procedure step by step. With precision, he casted and treated the child almost like a splendored crane winnowing to stand erect. He finished the procedure and winked at the boy. With great anticipation, the young boy exerted himself to a standing position and took a step. The residents were stunned at first, then reared up to applaud. JR paused for a brief second in the light.

He bowed to them and concluded, "Like you, I am a disciple of my profession. We are all actors in a much larger plan. Thank you."

He refocused his eyes on his fellows as they came up to the stage. His gaze drifted to catch view of Ayako. Next to her existed a shadow of a vision. He hastened to peer closer. His eyes and face flushed in disbelief. She was the image he had hoped to see again. He stepped forward to further inspect the unimagined apparition. Could it be?

It was Kami.

He excused himself to make his way to her. Ayako was standing behind her with both hands on her shoulders. Ayako unexpectedly spoke first. "You did leave something behind—my daughter."

"Ah," he said unashamedly and looked at Kami. "I want you so in my life."

With her characteristic smile she stated, "I am here. You have your match."

Until now, for him, for them both, this kind of certainty was never so clear. It was something he had not planned for. He had been successful in most everything he had set his mind to do. In his life, he considered marriage as a major step for him. He had believed he would be well established before it happened. He had never entertained a sense of who it would be, what was right, or where it would take place. He thought to call the priest back at Notre Dame Basilica. It was a practicality of his faith and belief. But, he already knew the unquestionable beauty of this pearl.

First, the major made a call to the local Catholic diocese. He reached an older priest. He explained his desires, the most immediate of which was to meet. The priest agreed to rendezvous at the church.

They met outside the steps of St. Ignatius. The priest immediately started, "You see this church behind me. It began with the Jesuit missionary Francis Xavier in 1549. It was built from the ashes of a simple chapel burned down during the great Tokyo air raid. It is now transformed into an international beacon that brings together many of all faiths." He motioned to walk the grounds. They entered a garden laced with cherry blossoms and a large oval pond. They walked over a bridge with floating lotus adrift below. The priest asked, "What is it that brings you here?"

JR spoke freely, "I am trying to discern all that has happened in my life." He went on, "My faith, my duty, my convictions, and change. What to hold onto and what to let go of."

The priest began, "I am glad you are in tune with these things. Often, one does not in his lifetime ask these questions." He continued, "I, too, was once like you. The age-old question, what does it mean to keep the faith? What makes up the balance of life's journey?" They walked a bit further, then stopped and sat on a stone bench. The priest continued. "Your faith is your root. It will always be your root. You were born into it and cannot deny it. It will carry forth since it will always be a part of you." He pointed farther out from the garden. "Look at that those two magnificent cypress trees. The Japanese call them *hinoki*. They are the most prized wood in all of Japan. If you look closely, it has a straight grain. It is considered a sacred wood with its directional strength and fragrant foliage. See all its branches. The tree was not aware of how its parts would sprout, much less the direction of its growth. All it knows is to reach toward the light and grow forth." He paused then continued, "Each tree has a root. Look how its trunk grows and its limbs intertwine with each other. It has created a connection apart from each limb's beginning. See it shedding a great canopy to the creatures below, creating nesting for the winged living in its middle, and its upper rising arched to heaven's reach."

JR nodded, but interjected. "I see, but Father, what is all this to do with my beliefs?"

He continued, "Now, think of the Savior. He was born a Jew, studied the sacred text as a Jew, and taught it back as a Jew. Yet, did he not grow in spirit and extend through the Father's grace all of the exemplary faith we have and see in the world today? And, yet, he even had to die for it so he could rise from it. This mystery continues." He went on, "If you come to Mass, every day I hold up the Eucharist. I see the Body of Christ rising within the branches of those two trees. I see the Blood of Christ in all beings who rise and intertwine together in the expanding branches. It is far reaching. It all is to be connected."

They each paused to reflect in their walk back to the front

of the church. The priest stated, "I hope I was of some help." JR followed, "I wish I would have known you before." He grinned and replied, "I wish I was a growing *hinoki*!"

As they turned to depart, the priest questioned, "Oh, one last thing. What is your fiancée's name?" JR said, "Kami." The priest then breathed, "Ah, yes." He revealed obligingly, "*Kami* is the sacred Japanese word for God." JR replied, "I see now."

JR thanked the priest and walked from the grounds. As he rounded the corner, he caught sight of the St. Ignatius Church welcome sign displaying the Mass hours. A small inscription underneath read:

You are loved. Peace is with you. Fr. Raphael

JR returned to the ryokan. He sat to pour out and sip the fresh tea he found on the table. He then slipped into the *onsen*. Upon entering, he could smell a pleasing fragrance in the wood. He marveled at its exquisite grained basin and lay back, adrift in a well sense of being. He spent the rest of the afternoon meditating outside in the bonsai garden. Later, he requested the use of a telephone. He wanted to make a call to his father and mother. Much had happened in Japan, not least his announced betrothal to Kami.

XXV

The wedding combined a richness of Eastern Japanese tradition with Western ways. A respect for and combination of customs beckoned consideration. Although they had both been raised Catholic, the broader sense of Catholicism was more elastic in its "universal" meaning. In fact, the marriage sacrament itself was quite alike in both cultures. An adaptation was welcomed on both sides of the Catholic-Shinto ceremony. For JR and Kami, the celebration would bridge the Eastern culture with the Western. Fr. Raphael of St. Ignatius and a Kannushi priest named Joo would concelebrate.

In the Shinto style, the bride wore a white kimono symbolizing purity and the blessing of family unity. Her silky black hair would be gathered and worn high within a white fan-like headdress called a *wataboshi*. A small sword and fan would be carried in her *obi* belt, representing a future of happiness. The groom wore a formal kimono in black. Isao mentioned, "Do you have a katana sword?" JR responded, "Well, yes, from my father. Although, it is back in America." Isao stood and offered, "Then you will have mine. It is from my father. And, I will have yours when I visit you."

Inclusive and mindful of the Catholic and Shinto traditions, Frs. Raphael and Joo agreed to insert sacred wedding ceremonial rituals as they presented. The procession would be in unison followed with a prayer, readings, and homily. The Catholic vows would take place in the honored fashion of choosing husband and wife, loving and trusting one other, the sharing of all times, blessings upon them and their families, and then the exchange of rings. Next came the Consecration including the Eucharistic Body and Blood with the purification of the nuptial cups.

Following, the Shinto vows took place. In the Shinto fashion, the couple drank sake three times from three different cups. The first sips represented the appreciation for their ancestry, the second sips the acknowledgment of human flaws and misgivings, and the third sips the freedom from flaws and the promise to take care of each other as long as they live. At the end, both recited a written prayer of gratitude, including service to one another and proclaimed love that would last for their lifetimes.

To conclude, Fr. Raphael blessed them and all in attendance. Priest Joo touched a material ornament on each of their shoulders, reflecting unity. Finally, the couple presented a prayer and a red rose to Mary and placed an evergreen twig on the altar as a gift in gratitude to God.

The afternoon reception was festive. Colorful sushi filled a table display with sea bream, prawns, red rice, and bean paste sweets. A new ceremonial barrel of sake was broken open. Traditional Japanese beer, rice wine, and Suntory whisky was alternately backstopped.

To the guests' surprise, in departing, Kami threw a bouquet of chrysanthemums that landed in Sutibu's lap. Everyone laughed. The departing gift to the couple was a *mizuhiki* knot in the shape of a crane.

JR spoke up, "What does this mean?" Kami answered,

"Cranes mate for life." She continued, "They stand for good for-tune, longevity, and peace in marriage." She paused and carried on, "Only one thing is left." JR spoke, "What is that?" Kami turned to JR, "When we return to America, we will celebrate again for those not here. But, know that I marry you every day." JR replied, "And I you."

XXVI

The Nippon Foundation was pleased to report to the major a range of treatment protocols they had derived from his presentation. They needed his approval for future implementation. JR and Kami were called in to see Reiko, Isao, and Ayako.

What was unexpected in their meeting was the presence of a USMC military officer. He was immediately recognized as Captain Beckwith. JR and Kami immediately saluted. He was a known field commander in Vietnam, decorated in military service and accomplishments. He began, "I am here today to award you the distinguished medal for service in health and human services." He stepped forward and pinned it to the major's lapel. The captain continued, "As a token of your loyalty and confidence above and beyond the cause of your enlisted mission, I am pleased to reenact your civilian status and file honorable discharge papers relieving you from your duties."

The major was taken back. He spoke, "With permission, sir, our duty was short lived in our service." The captain responded, "Maybe short lived, but long lasting in effect." He then winked and replied, "That is the best kind."

They shook hands. The major's eyes watered. He thought of his father. An emotion of pride swelled in him for his country. The captain walked away and then suddenly turned to speak further. "Oh, and one last thing." He paused, "This also applies to your wife. Have a nice honeymoon."

The newlyweds rented an apartment off of Nogizaka Station. It conveniently routed through the megapolis of Grand Tokyo Station. After World War II, Tokyo had had the chance to rebuild itself into an efficient model of urban city living. For one, automobile usage was not encouraged nor planned. The subway network played an intricate display in modern travel under and above ground. Its advanced design introduced a mass flow model for the urbanized world's admiration. The train maps tangled like octopus tentacles directing its arms into a squeezed space of mobility. Shinto shrines were principled near every subway stop much like American churches were prescribed at a city's busiest intersection. Since they had no mode of personal motorized transportation, most locals traversed around via foot or the preferred plethora of bicycles. As throughout Japan's developing cities, Tokyo practically mandated its population to honor this rule of urban life. With its convenient mercantile markets and stopwatch-precise transport timing, the city embodied the world's debut definition of metropolis.

Being in the military, JR and Kami were already familiar with tight quarters. Here, housing was set up much the same to maximize space. The apartments allowed for Western beds, yet they could be folded into the walls for added space utilization. The kitchen was located in the living area. It consisted of a refrigerator, sink, table for grilling, rice cooker, and electric teakettle. The only sliding divider was between the bathroom and stackable washer and dryer, when available.

The most unique conservation feature was the toilet. It included a pop-up waterspout at the back of the tank's top surface. This water stream could be used to cleanse hands and then spill over to fill the toilet. The washer and dryer were plumbed to perform the same. Practicality was the norm as they witnessed an archetype of a dynamic society constantly on the move.

They decided to make foot to the Meiji Shrine. As they got close, they could see the landmark 1964 Olympic stadium. What they had not accounted for was the evergreen forest rambling across the center of the city. Their path led them to an immense tori gate. Its girth and height represented a significant chapter for Japan. It was a crossover between the island's feudal history of shogun rule and the vision of Emperor Meiji to unify all of Japan. It reminded the couple of their marriage. Two pillars standing strong apart but connected to a greater source above.

Kami stopped before passing through and bowed. JR politely asked, "Why do you bow?" Kami answered, "Consider it like genuflecting before you enter church. The tori gate is considered the entrance to a sacred place." As they walked further, the route was laced with lanterns illuminating the way. Sika deer would come out of the forest and stoop between the stone columns and Kami would step up and bow to them. Remarkably, the deer would tip its antler rack down in return as if cued.

Intrigued by the two foreigners, an elder Japanese man with a crooked cane made his way to JR's side. He observed Kami as well. Still wondering at the deer JR muttered to himself, "What is this? How is it that they wander free unafraid here?" The elder cleared his voice to make his presence known and turned to JR saying in broken English, "It is believed that our ancestry lives within these living spaces." JR looked at him and could see the passage of time on his face. The elder continued, "The shrine considers the visitation of the deer as sacred. They are a part of our beliefs. All are honored and considered a treasure from the divine."

JR then spoke up to the elder. "Hmm, forgive me, but what if one of the deer is hunted and killed?"

The other responded, "Before the Meiji, it was considered a capital offense punishable by death." He went on, "We have no guns in Japan. The police wear no guns. All disputes are settled in nonthreatening ways. It is very difficult to live in peace if non-peaceful means are obtained. These are the rules."

"But surely," JR responded, "If you need to live by taking a food source, what is one to do?"

"Certainly." The elder paused, then sighed and continued, "If a life is taken, then you give back to the life."

"I do not understand."

The man pointed. "You see over there? A man eats a fish. And over there, a fish is being released back into the water. And there, another man eats rice. And there, a man plants seeds of rice in the field."

JR courteously nodded to the elder in understanding and walked over to Kami. She smiled and pranced as free as the deer. She slipped her hand into his. They leisurely made their way to the main shrine. To the left, he could see a decorative water basin with ladles hanging around it.

The elder man once again appeared. He brushed by saying in a low tone, "See and follow." He went up to the long trough and took a ladle into his right hand. He scooped it into the water to pour some over his left hand to rinse. He switched the ladle to his left to rinse his right. He then poured water into his hand and sipped to rinse his mouth. Finally, he switched the ladle back to his right hand to rinse his left again. He eased the ladle vertical to allow the remaining water to spill out. He returned the ladle to its resting place.

Next, he walked up to the shrine and stood underneath a tree trunk-size twisted straw bough. He pulled on a vertical rope from which a bell clanged. It was if he attempted to awaken an indweller. He threw a token into a slotted offertory-type box. He bowed twice and then clapped twice. He pressed his hands together at chin level in a fashion to pray. After a solemn time, he stepped back, bowed once, and clapped once. After all this he walked back to JR. "Now you do the same. It is Shinto custom."

For many, the Meiji transformation of the old to new thrusted society into the present. However, the indigenous ancient religion was firmly rooted in all Japanese everyday life. No original founder, no holy book to be found, no concept of religious conversion. Simply, it presented a harmony in existence with nature and the virtue of a sincere heart.

The elder made his way to Kami as if he knew something was different about her. He asked her name. "Ahh," he spoke, "I see now." He paused and continued. *"Kami* in Shinto means 'divine spirit.' The name is found in mythology, nature, and human beings. Japanese people feel the awe and gratitude to dedicate shrines to them." He smiled to her and bowed. He then took her hand and led her to the hand of her husband.

Before going on his way, he turned to muster a last word. "When you leave here, you leave a sacred place like no other." He went on, "Please understand." He paused. "You have walked among trees planted by hand for hundreds of years."

JR and Kami walked through the forested park. They found a place to lie on their backs. Here they pondered the view through the crown of the trees. It seemed new, old, and familiar to JR somehow. They were shadowed in the warm misting moisture exhumed from the canopy of trees. The humidity of the drenched air permeated through their clothes to make contact with skin. It was almost as if they were bathing amongst the forest trees.

JR closed his eyes, mindful of each breath and of the mystical shower of nature's cleansing. He reflected back to his leisure time during childhood. He used to take comfort in reading Mark Twain novels. Often, he would take a book and sit on a dell cliff perched high off the Great Lake of Michigan. He thought back to the author's words and his characters' adventures abroad. They brought to mind where he was now. He remembered a quote used at the end of Twain's travelogue. He spoke it aloud now. *"Travel is fatal to prejudice, bigotry, and narrow-mindedness."* He had witnessed and comprehended something quite grand. He turned to Kami and said, "I see now. I'm glad we came."

The forest exited into an area of rowed cherry trees. It was a cemetery. It lured the two in. Aoyama Cemetery was the largest public cemetery in all of Japan. Here, Japanese headstones were at rest alongside foreigners' graves. The display of stone lanterns, pagodas, and shrines abided throughout while Christian symbols and crosses coexisted as well. The pink-blossomed trees lined the grounds in fashionable order. JR thought it most mimicked Arlington Cemetery in Washington, D.C. The two gazed upon the engraved stones planted in the space before them. Blanketing the acreage, they showed names of German, Dutch, French, and English lineage as well as naturalized Japanese-American.

Kami suddenly spoke up. "This is where I need to return to at the end of our time." Confused and astonished, JR followed with, "What are you saying? Is there something you need to tell me?"

They found a place to nestle into between a Buddha statue and tori gate. She began, "I was born in America's Arizona. My mother Ayako was traveling with her husband to visit the land he was raised upon. They met during the war and married. He was not able to return. My mother told me he fell ill and died in America. She had not been able to meet his family." JR reached to hold her hand. She continued, "At the time, she had nowhere to go and no way to return home. She sought refuge in a thriving Japanese community based in California. They assisted her with food and shelter." She paused. "I was born there. Even though my father had been a patriot of the United States, my mother did not have the proper papers to reside there. She made plans for me to stay. She felt it was my best chance for a better life than what might lie ahead for me in Japan. She secretly deported herself back to her homeland one night." She sighed and went on. "A new family and friends helped raise me. We spent five years in a Japanese internment camp. It was there I learned my English and Catholic faith. I worked in the vegetable fields and studied hard.

When I was older, I applied to medical school. I had the grades but was rejected because of my race and gender. So I learned about physical therapy. It allowed another way. It was my way to serve. It was a way to connect with my mother." She then breathed deeply and looked up. "A way to connect back to Japan. Mostly, another way to connect with you." She took his other hand. She embraced him and said, "Thank you." JR whispered, "Always." Suddenly, he jumped up enthusiastically and promptly lifted Kami up as well. "Come on, let's have some fun!"

They stepped into the areas of Shibuya and Shinjuku. They were known for their restaurants and entertainment. JR and Kami could smell the flamed *hibachi* meat grills. *Wagyu* or *Kobe*, a marbled beef known for its succulent nature, melted in one's mouth even before chewing. They passed a small windowed eatery with a sumo-looking woman inside flipping heaping mounds of cabbage, noodles, seaweed, egg, fish, meats, vegetables, and more. The combination appeared irresistible. They looked at each other for the eyed gastronomical okay. Then they nodded to reverse course and take a seat at the diner.

"Konnichiwa! *Desu Okonomiyaki?*" the owner proclaimed to his new guests. The translation resembled, "Hello! You'll like my food!" They gave a resounding "Hai!" The dish concoction they received was referred to as the soul food of Japan. Its base consisted of a crepe or pancake of puréed yam, shredded cabbage, and flour. From there a smorgasbord of green onion, meats, octopus, squid, shrimp, vegetables, and cheese would be grilled and "Fuji'd"' up. For that matter anything could be added on top. It was a fun way to eat.

Afterward, they headed to the new opening of the talked-about robot bonanza show. From the entrance, the place shimmered with glass, mirrors, and glittery gold. They entered an obscene and decadent cornucopia of lights, smoke, sound, gizmo robots, decorative animals, and outrageous actors in flamboyant attire. A musical odyssey of sound effects would blast through the creative floating spaceships at the fire from the monster Godzilla. Following poured a horde of flying techno-tin raptors engaged with trapeze-interlocking monkeys swinging and diving in contorted positions. In finale, a release of bubbles, balloons, and birds into the audience raised the mayhem. It was an indoor extravaganza of pure outrageous fantasy.

They had not had so much fun in their whole lives. It felt like the official start to their honeymoon. Without the reminder of time, the evening slipped into morning hours. They thought it best to complete the night in a hotel. But all were taken. The only remaining were the capsule hotels. It was obvious that Tokyo had unique provisions.

A capsule, known as a "pod," had been introduced in Japan. It was a way station for no-frills sleep. What was so exotic was the arrangement: Each pod measured only one by one by three meters. They were stacked upon each other like Legos. The couple found pods that would fit each person separately. Kami declared, "Well, that's not what I had in mind!" According to rules of etiquette, men and woman had separated quarters. Nonetheless, late in the morning JR smuggled his bride in disguise into the cramped quarters, primarily for good humor and also to challenge the possibility of squeezing in another.

Suddenly, there was a knock at the door. "Sir, you have broken the rules and must leave immediately or be fined." Little had they expected, the antic was not appreciated. They politely scurried away with a humorous experience to remember. It was the end of a full day's experience as the sun rose into the next.

Sensoji was the last place they decided to visit in Tokyo before moving on. It was the oldest Buddhist temple in the city. It had survived the war bombings and fires. They made their way to the structure. A large barrel of burning incense was centered at the entrance. A heavy wave of fragrance filled the air. The customary ritual included fanning it through one's being in an act of cleansing and purification. More often, the result was a self-induced coughing fit.

At the top of the steps directly inside the temple sat a revering Buddha, and to the side stood the delicate statuary of the Bodhisattva of Compassion. Kami went to sit quietly on her knees in front of the statuary. JR stepped back from the pouring crowds to remain at a respectful distance. To him, a panoramic view of the temple offered a grander sweep. His mind returned to the reverent churches, basilicas, and chapels of his youth. It somehow reflected a central sense of sacrificial tolerance with Our Lady's temperance at the fulcrum. He pondered how suffering had become such an inescapable passage to living. Why it was so necessary. He excused himself into the outside air. He could see in the distance one tori reflecting a cross-like image in its column. For the first time, he wondered if it was all just the same.

He felt a tug. Kami placed her arm around him and asked, "What are you thinking?" JR said, "I am pondering all the similarities. It seems throughout all of history, one nation's ways trumps in its reign upon over another. I can't see how it is not one. Maybe there is room for it all." Kami responded, "When I was a child, my adopted father would ask me to sit and to breathe in and out. He then asked me to listen to the words coming from my breath. At first, I could not perceive. I tried harder and harder the older I got. Still I could not. Then one evening I just let go. I sat as quietly as I could. In my inhaled breath I could hear 'Yaaahhhh,' and in my exhaled breath 'Wehhhh.' It seems that all our lives we are on a human journey to know and comprehend God." She continued, "Maybe we needlessly suffer because we lose focus of this simple presence. Whether it is suffering on a cross to reveal salvation or becoming enlightened through a spiritual path, we are all sentient travelers here. It is important to contemplate, pray, and meditate on all the same."

They wandered back into the surround of Ueno Park. Ameyko, as it was called, was a flurry of open-air markets originally known for the line of candy stores and sugary treats since postwar times. More recently, it was known for its surplus of army goods. Now it had over five hundred shops selling products of fresh food, cloth, anime, and pearls. JR and Kami were hand-locked in the fray of exchanges so not to be separated from each other. The Japanese macaque advertised their presence by handing out treats from their perch on the shoulders of shopkeepers. Lollipop anime girls and colorfully garbed geishas presented themselves. Flapping fish and squirreling octopus on sticks sizzled over the charcoal stands. It was a grand bazaar in Tokyo that would launch them into their next adventure.

XXVII

Kami and JR had a vested interest in traveling to the Kyushu province. Both had ties to family history there. In the honeymooning time they had left, they would entrench themselves in the culture of the land. The affordable spoils from Ameyko allowed each to travel light. Their first step was to master the "bullet" transportation system.

The Shinkansen was a marvel the world had not yet seen. It was started during the Olympics of 1964 and developed into the fastest ever mass transit system connecting Japan's vast prefectures. Its purpose was to assist in economic growth and development. Many workers in the capital city would live in faraway regions and commute through this network. The engine design was built in the shape of a flat-tipped bullet to run at speeds of 200 miles per hour. Frequently, the trains raced to 275 miles per hour on long stretches. Sixteen trains per hour carried 15,000 passengers in and out of Tokyo alone. Its albatross reached to the corners of the country.

A massive billboard in the central station displayed all the departure and arrival times met with punctual precision. The decision to optimize roadways had given way to the train rail systems burrowing between the mountains of the islands. Through the impetuousness of the conductors, three minutes were scheduled between trains with pointers painted on the ground in plain sight to aid speedy, systematic boarding on and off. JR and Kami bought tickets for a sweeping excursion through the western Honshu prefecture. It would take three hours to their first stop. Here they would encounter their first adventure.

The views out the windows were breathtaking. They swept around the mountain interplay between the majestic Fuji and the Pacific shores. It was a geological cornucopia. The ocean buoyed the rise of the Earth's crust to a snow-tipped point. You could imagine the origin of the deity worship folklore from ancient times. The breath and speed of the train felt similar to a wingless plane racing down a runway and attempting never-accomplished lift. The rush past coastline was dotted with manufacturing facilities, with signage indicating companies from Sony to Toyota.

As the train made an effortless corner around to Okayama, unexpectedly, a loud shriek of pumped breaks was heard and felt. Then, a discernible thud. A dark-colored blob tumbled over the train's nose bridge. JR jumped. "What the h—— was that!" The bullet transport came to a stop. The intercom barked a phrase in Japanese followed by the English: "All exit. Emergency stop!"

JR and Kami disembarked to view the bullet nose crunched, with loose hair sticking to the expansive windshield. "What happened?" JR posed. The conductor replied, "Unfortunate collision with hairy-legged beast on tracks. Train down. You will have to walk from here." JR followed, "Does this often happen?" The other said, "Very rare. Only when hoofs get stuck in between tracks. This way please."

They grabbed their items and exited into rain. Covering their heads they walked to the terminal a mile away. As they boarded the platform, JR realized that the next train would be blocked if the first one was not attended to by the engineers soon enough. He turned to Kami and urged, "Let's rent a car."

JR was able to rent a car. However, he could not anticipate what he found inside when he opened the door. In Japan, the rules of driving were the reverse of what he was accustomed to. The driving was on the left side of the road. Thus, the steering column was on the right, with stick shift on his left. It would take him a while to master a smooth coordinated drive. He practiced in the parking lot first. Then he tested his skills around the block. Kami was sure to be his navigator so not to revert the new habit.

They drove up into the mountainside of western Honshu. Their destination was a small town called Kagamino, shy of Mount Daisen. In town, they were to meet a contact of Ayako who would offer them shelter and respite. His home would be marked with a green winged slate roof. They pulled into the town and caught sight of it. As they entered the private grounds, a pepper-haired man with a beard greeted them. The familiar greetings were made in welcoming each other. The man said, "I am Debbido, father of Ayako." Kami was unaware she had a grandfather. "Come in," he offered.

"I have built this by hand," he continued. The design of the home was woven with bonsai, lanterns, and koi ponds. Unique were the angled gutters, running with water. The heavy misted mountain forest air funneled moisture into a central cedar basin. "You must be tired and thirsty." He continued, "Please, drink from the waters of my home." JR ladled a cup of water for Kami and himself. "Delicious," they chimed. They had never tasted water so pure. Debbido went on, "I have Wagyu for tonight. Bring your things to the room I have prepared."

They entered the abode. A small delicate shrine was above the foyer inside, inciting a bow of welcome from the visitors. Similar to the tori, striking vertical timbers crossed into horizontal supports above their heads. Sliding doors with screens of delicate paper tracked smoothly in grooves to separate rooms. A central sitting area had a fire pit recessed into the cedar floor planking. A kettle floated above it, hung by a twisted rope. Debbido gestured to sit.

"You are my guests. It is time for tea." A fragrant tea was poured from the kettle and savored by all. The smell of rice and vegetables steaming in a cooker wafted to their nostrils. Their host stirred a fire in the pit and fanned it to sear the Wagyu steaks placed on. He finger-pressed them to tender with dark pink color throughout, as characteristic of Japanese cooking standards.

"Before we eat, we must toast." He conveyed, "We make our own sake here. It comes from the best natural mountain waters, rice, and fungi in all of Japan." JR enjoyed sake, but had no idea of the complexity in the process of brewing it. So Debbido explained. The fermentation of alcohol in wine or beer happens in introducing the grape sugars to yeast. However, sake is not fermented by adding yeast to rice. Koji, a fungus microorganism culture, is added to rinsed, soaked rice. It is then steamed and mashed to begin an enzymatic process. These enzymes convert the starch from the rice into sugar. The yeast uses the sugar to create alcohol fermentation. It is then pressed, filtered, pasteurized, and aged before bottling.

Debbido presented the drink on a ceramic tray with handle-less cups. He poured the sake slowly with a precise tilt of a side-spouted stone ladle. It displayed a delicate "v" stream into the cups. He took and raised his cup with both hands in gesture.

"JR," he said, "it is customary and honorable for first guest to toast!" JR, somewhat unprepared, said what came most quickly to mind. "Kanpai!" The three laughed, drank, and then ate in delight.

"Before we retire, we perform *Waka*." Debbido continued, "This is the way you will gift me with your gratitude and something to remember you by." JR and Kami looked at each other. They had no idea what he was speaking of. In seeing their confusion, he explained, "Waka is traditional Japanese poetry. You leave your spirit truth in a poem." Observing intrigued faces, he went on, "You will write a poem of five lines: five syllables in the first, followed by seven, five, seven, and finally seven. I will give you calligraphy pens and fine rice paper for its keeping. You have only five minutes, since you must speak from the heart. I will do this as well." They nodded in approval of this attempt. They closed their eyes before writing. Then they put pen to paper. When the time ended, they each laid out their poems. Debbido spoke. "I will read mine first, JR's second, and Kami's third." He started:

> I walk on the path
> Everything has space now
> I pause to reflect
> Meditate for clarity
> Many roads lead to heaven.

Then he continued:

> When I contemplate
> Compassion is in your smile
> It is usual
> The greatest gift of one's life
> Ever present in your face.

And further:

> Lift up your spirit
> Awaken to become more
> Truth is all around
> One naturally aware
> Giving kindness matters most.

And he concluded, "Arigato. Thank you for celebrating your noble birth in Waka. In the morning, I will ask just one thing in labor before you depart. Good night."

In the morning, he greeted them with rubber boots on. The countryside before them was swept with tiered rice fields. Men and women would stand in tall rubber boots in a pod and they would adjust the water channels with sliding guillotine doorstops. It regulated the mountain stream's flow into the fields. They then measured the depths of saturation with a marked stick. With that, rice pad growth could be measured and harvesting could be determined.

Debbido expressed, "These are my field workers. They rake now to harvest a plot of rice." He smiled. "This row is ready." JR questioned, "How do you know?" The other stated, "The water tells us." JR remarked, "Please, go on."

Debbido continued, "We direct the mountain water streams into these flat, tiered plots filled with seedlings and fertilizer in the spring. Then we fill with water to the measure of five inches deep. It allows the rice to stabilize and compete against weeds for nutrients and sunlight. As it matures, long panicles are seen on top of the plant. It can reach a height of three feet. It is imperative to mark the water at five inches and run excess into the tier below to repeat." JR looked at the smattering of long grains in one field and none in the next. He asked, "Why is there no water in this field?" Debbido responded, "Because this field has perfectly ripe grain. It has been drained. The harvester tractor is ready to bring the grains to the trailer alongside."

Debbido then surprised them with a question. "Can you both drive in a straight line?" JR and Kami nodded. He continued, "Good, then I will need your service." With that, Debbido directed JR into the harvester and instructed him in its operation. Kami would drive alongside in the collection wagon. With this kind of teamwork, they could sweep out the rice gently and rapidly into bins.

The couple plowed forward. They looked back after a one-pass clearing. They promptly high-fived each other on a mission accomplished. They could see Debbido channeling water back into the fields. They looked with great interest now since the field had been harvested. Circling into the newly created shallows were cranes, ducks, and geese. They landed, grateful for the porridge of broken-down rice straw and mud crustaceans.

Two tons of rice were cleared that morning. Little had they ever imagined leaving America in the call of duty to turn to the call of Japanese rice harvesting.

In the end, Debbido provided fresh rice in rolls of sushi for their continuing journey. Before parting he turned to JR. "JR," he said, "in America, is that name not the meaning of the junior of your father?" JR responded, "Well, yes, I guess it is." The other replied, "That is good."

He then turned his attention to Kami. "You are as beautiful as the sun setting over Japan. You must rise over Kokura where your ancestry began." She bowed and then embraced her grandfather. JR paused for a moment and quietly murmured, "Kokura," remembering his father. As they pulled away, they could still see Debbido standing from a distance. Kami held a prolonged stare with her distinctive smile. She sighed, "Look at all the cranes behind him."

To the north was not the typical route for foreign travelers. From Kagamino, they could see a mountain peak at a great distance. Most followed the populous path along the shores of the Pacific. But their spirit took them higher.

They arrived at the base of Mount Daisen. It was next to the highest mountain in Japan, outside of Fuji. It was very approachable and climbable in the right season. There existed an approach on its inside volcanic fissure. It would allow them to hike the five thousand-foot summit. They decided to take it. Kami remarked, "Oh, the air is so fresh and clean." She went on, "Look at the mountain rocks with water dripping into a gentle stream." JR came over to see the water stream down a boulder's face. He went over and cupped his hands for a drink. "There is nothing like it. The sake of the Earth."

XXVIII

The foot traffic on the mount was sparse except for surefooted monks on a select pilgrimage of some sort. Sure enough, the couple came upon a Buddhist temple built on the slopes. A monk approached and warned them, "This is the shrine on the mountain of the great god. You cannot go further except with a monk." It was unexpected but somewhat welcomed due to the terrain's ruggedness and the whims of the great elevation. A female monk in white robes walked up and addressed them. "My name is Mommi. I am Shugendo. I can be of service."

JR and Kami were delighted and surprised by her English. JR responded, "We are interested in getting to the top."

"Very well," she said but explained further, "I can help you, but you must help me." They were intrigued and waited for more. She continued, "I am a mountain ascetic and we have rules in our syncretic ways here."

JR responded, "Please explain?"

"We have been in these mountains of Japan since year 700." Mommi continued, "Shugendo is our path to spiritual power through discipline and testing. It is the amalgamation of Buddhism, Shintoism, and more. The Meiji rule tried to separate them for order. We see it as syncretism. It is a way that incorporates many religions for the sake of self-discipline and enlightenment."

JR stated, "I see. How does that apply here?"

"Be aware that trials exist along the way that illustrate the Shugendo training I have described. These reflect the spiritual journey which tests the nature of the strongest of us. Shall we proceed?"

She led them upward on a narrow path. The scenery was breathtaking with the majestic peak view ahead underplayed by a treacherous slide down. She turned at a bridge crossing, saying, "You will see the first test of the monks." She went on, "The sacred mountain teaches us about our capacity to suffer and endure human trials."

They cornered around a precipice and saw that they were heading to a waterfall and another bridge crossing. As they approached, they could see a monk on the stone bridge looking down at the waterfall below. There, six monks were disrobed and in water up to the neck. The falls pounded on their heads as they treaded lightly with eyes closed. It looked like a state of chilled consciousness. The three quietly walked across the bridge without a sound.

Heading higher, they witnessed the beginning of another event. A sort of twisted rope they so often had observed at Shinto shrines was laid out in length, disappearing over the edge of a cliff. As they stepped up toward the rock face and peered from their great height, they could see a monk with the rope tied in a loop around one foot. Five monks were holding to the other end as the monk descended down the cliff face. He orientated himself by feeling surfaces with his hands, feet, and body to check positioning. He held firmly to the surface ledges and cracks as he belayed downward. JR and Kami sat for a moment to observe the acrobatic feat.

Suddenly, the man lost his bearings and fell. The five monks attempted to hold the line at the other end. However, they began slipping in their traction. JR, Kami, and Mommi instantly rushed to grab hold with the five to assist. The monk swung by one ankle far above the ground, soundless in his teetering state. From overhead the monks sounded aloud, "*Sensou*, sensou, sensou!" Mommi looked over at the couple and interpreted, "Hold, hold, and hold!" Mustering all their strength, they held their position and place. The sweat ran down their faces as the man's fate dangled in the air.

JR cried, "We need to pull him up! We can't do this forever." The monks recanted, "Sensou!" Suddenly, the line became less tense. The holders relaxed. Relieved JR asked, "What happened?" Mommi stated, "He connected back to the rock's surface." She explained, "It is part of the training. All require patient fortitude."

They reached the peak. Mommi reached into her side bag and brought out a conch shell. She puckered into it, barreling out a bass tone which echoed through the forest below. She then crouched and recited a long chant. The words were in harmony with the motions of her legs and arms as they rhythmically flowed with the gentle wind. Afterwards, she bowed to the vastness. JR stepped to the cliff edge to take a look. He could then see the magnificent horizon of sunlit valleys, ravines, and mountain lakes reflected off the Sea of Japan.

Mommi turned to them and spoke. "You have traveled the way of Shugendo. It is the way of gods. It is the path of deity."

JR interrupted to ask, "Why the rituals of tests, horn, chants, and chi?"

"It is to remind us of our true nature. That we must return to it. This way, we return to ourselves." She continued, "It is here you begin asking who you really are. In all that you test on the mountain, you will find answers to your questions."

They began the descent, this time in silence and mindfulness.

As they rounded to the temple, they could see a bonfire before it. Many monks were circled around it, lighting torches as if in commencing a ceremony. They formed a line and walked down a path of tall, canopied cedars. They handed bamboo torches to JR, Kami, and Mommi for them to follow in procession. As they walked through the grand trees, JR and Kami watched the smoke and light ahead mystically undulating beneath the surface of the overhanging leaves. Supernatural images emanated from it, depicting many swirling, interactive illusions in succession. They felt a subtle euphoria in the ceremonial harmony which grounded the ritual in the mountainous nature. At the end, Mommi said she had to leave. She had to return to her monastic community. JR reached in his pocket to pay her for her guidance. She placed her hand on his forearm before he could retrieve any yen. She said simply, "Cherish the entire universe and pray for peace."

It was not long before they found their car. They sat in it for a while, transfixed by what they had experienced off the beaten track. They were hesitant to leave, as if subconsciously unwrapping a well-meant secret. They were content in a feeling of resolve. A feeling of how they were to achieve awareness, heightened clarity, and pure connection through a new alternative way. They had experienced something that soulfully resided in the less traveled mountains.

They headed south to take the exit road to the Pacific Honshu coast. They nixed the bullet train. It was too fast for what they hoped to see more of. Up ahead, the change lanes guided them toward Hiroshima. It was an unexpected detour unable to be avoided.

JR recalled his father again. Japan's surrender had seemed predicated on the use of atomic weaponry in a hurry to end a war. He wondered whether the planned invasion by the Russians invading through Korea would have been any better for the Allied cause. His military training had led him to know that the positional chess playing between the Americans and Russians would not have a good outcome. But, when it was done, it was the Americans who had set the stage for an ambitious democracy.

XXIX

Hiroshima stood as a city once buried in 1945 to a bustling metropolis of skyscrapers these thirty years later. Upon entering, the main highway led to Peace Memorial Park, which seemingly no roads avoided. It was an eerie sight, this city with showcased reminders of what had been, what never should happen again, and what utopia looked like ahead. A walking lane persuaded them into the heart of the park along the Ota River. They strolled around the back entrance to stumble upon the Genbaku Dome. It was ground zero, better known as the A-Bomb Dome. It was difficult to imagine the extent of the explosion fifteen hundred feet above the canopy they now walked under. No doubt, the locals in 1945 had been just as unaware without the warning sound of an air raid.

They were surprised to see a Peace Pagoda in the shape of a Buddhist stupa. It was built and donated in honor of the Indian peace marcher Gandhi. Further away was the Memorial Cathedral for World Peace, the church built by a Jesuit missionary who was wounded in the blast. It seemed many faiths were reassuring solidarity in the mission for world peace.

"JR!" Kami exclaimed. "Today is the annual memorial ceremony!" They could see the long memorial walkway ablaze in purple-blue chrysanthemums and yellow roses. They hurried to take a chair. A distinguished man walked up to the memorial podium and began to speak:

"Thirty years ago, we witnessed the work of man;

The destruction of human life;

Here the death of countless people.

Nowhere is this truth more forcefully imposed upon than here in Hiroshima.

Here represents the beginning of the end,

This city is our poster child of the end of civilization.

It reflects the ill fortune of destruction beyond belief.

It is in our psyches forever.

Yet, it is here where the world comes and future generations gather to build world peace.

That too, is our destiny. A constant flame and hope for humanity."

Clapping interrupted as he added, "As a reminder, we now present to the world the Clock of Humanity." He raised the object up for all to see. "It will forever remind us of that second when this nuclear destruction occurred. Time will be kept each moment after to distance the destructive force from us. A timely reminder in renewed hope and commitment to never allow it to occur again, anywhere. From this moment on, we begin a new worldwide consciousness against war."

A standing applause erupted as hundreds of doves were released in a delegate synchrony. To the onlookers, the birds symbolized the promised harbingers of freedom.

JR was stunned. He had never heard such a speech. It raised the bar of hope for all mankind to work out any differences void raising the barrel of a weapon. To him, it conveyed significance for the country he believed in and ideals he fought for.

He turned to Kami. "Do you think freedom is possible despite race, creed, and nationality? Can we really live with one another and sit at this table of peace despite the privileged powerful forces around?" Kami put her arms around JR and said, "You mean, can truth transcend power?" She paused and continued, "Truth is always based in peace."

They heard a gong ring. They looked skyward from the processional walkway to see a large bell. It was the Peace Bell. A line of adults with children gathered around it quietly singing a melodic song.

They walked down the long corridor of the park and made their way back to the dome. They rested on an empty bench. JR looked around at the haunting dilapidated scorch of the scene. His father came to mind once again. He thought of all the fathers, sons, and daughters who had endured all types of suffering. How they existed now to remake themselves in some other way back to meaning.

A young boy was tossing a stick for his dog to fetch. The piece of wood landed at JR's feet. He reached to pick it up before the dog got to it. The dog sat down patiently two feet away. JR smiled at the boy and tossed the stick. The dog raced to catch it in midair and returned it to him.

The boy moved closer to JR. He started to notice a slight limp in the boy's walk as he sat on the ground near to him. Sure enough, as his trousers receded from his shoe, JR noticed an artificial foot and leg.

The boy took liberties and addressed him English. "Hi!"

JR followed, "Hi!" He went on, "What is your dog's name?"

"Yuki."

"He is a fine pet and great retriever." The boy nodded and JR continued, "What kind of dog is he?"

The boy responded, "Akita. Mountain dog."

The dog parked himself between the two. It seemed he created a bridge for them to speak. "So," JR continued, "I had a dog, too, back where I came from."

"Oh," said the boy. "Then he must be waiting for you."

JR responded, "Well, yes, I suppose so."

The boy went on, "My dog waits for me wherever I go." Then he continued with, to the surprise of their ears, "When I die, he will wait for me." He carried on, "When I was born, I was given a statue of an Akita. When I got older, my parents told me that the statue symbolized health, happiness, and afterlife. So, now I have a real one and I know."

Kami smiled. "Thank you for telling us your story."

He stood up and Yuki perked up to bark. "Well," he said. "I must go now." Then he surprised both of them again with his next words. "He is my angel in fur."

JR smiled and replied, "Yes. Sayonara, young friend. Until we meet again."

Located in the Seto Inland Sea, just outside Hiroshima, lay a most unusual place they heard of. The locals described it as an island where people and gods lived together. Miyajima Island had long been a sacred getaway for the Japanese, and for good reason. It reflected the best of Japan's nature. Getting there was mostly by ferry or boat. For the adventurous two, kayaks would be the alternative.

XXX

It was a calm morning. The ocean kayaks were pointed into the unperturbed waters of the bay. If they followed the trail of the ferryboat, they would arrive within one hour. They prepared the floating crafts for the adventure. Kami said, "It is wonderful to be on the water again." JR beamed and replied, "Agreed. Shove off!" They paddled the kayaks a distance behind the ferry in its smooth wake.

It was much like a cardio workout for them as they had performed in training. Now they welcomed the fun component of a familiar discipline. As they made tracks, they were struck by the composition of the residential shore structures. Most had a concrete water ramp that opened to the sea. It was for launching their fishing boats. Here, much of the industry was simply of man and fish. The locals and sea coexisted for the benefit of the other. The fishermen already at bay waved to the kayakers' non-disturbing wake. Even though they had no maritime map, the island could not be missed due to its imposing vermillion-hued landmark.

They paused in the bay to take in the view of the massive,

vibrant tori. Its imposing entrance hovered above the water at a height of sixteen meters. As they got closer, the predictable idea passed through JR's mind. He summoned Kami. "Let's go through."

An approach from other kayakers got their attention. A European couple enthusiastically calling joined them from the shoreline. Delighted, JR and Kami heard them speaking English. "G'day," the man said. He was answered in kind. JR remarked, "Isn't this something?" indicating the tori. "For sure, bloke," said the man. Somewhat befuddled by his unusual use of English, JR posed, "Where are you from?" The other boasted out, "Straya!" "Where?" came the question again. "Australia!" bellowed his paddling mate, "And no doubt you are Americans!"

"My name is Michael," the man introduced himself. "My mate's Nanette." JR and Kami responded with their own names. Kami began, "What brings you here?" Nanette replied, "Oh, we're stoked to live here." JR questioned, "Here?" "Yes," she said. "The island is a beaut!"

JR paddled close to Kami and started giggling. He said discreetly under his breath, "Beware these Aussies, you can see they have a language and style all of their own. This should be a hoot!"

As they paddled under the gate, Michael resumed, "The lay about say this is the edge between the spooky and the heads-up world. It's trippy but magical. Wouldn't you say, mate?" JR smiled and then chuckled into his hand. Michael continued, "It is up tide now, but soon it will be low. Either way, the tori will upper up! You should take a jaunt out later." JR posed a word in edgewise. "How does it stand?" Michael replied in his unfaltering slangy way, "At under tide, they diggity-dig to bury the strut in the salty bed. Then load up on stone to yackety-yak up. Peachy, eh?"

Kami and JR continued to paddle giggling toward the island's shore. As they disembarked, Michael shouted to the couple, "Well, we have to shoot through now, but maybe a frothy later?" They smiled and gave the thumbs-up as the Australians continued onward. Unexpectedly, a four-legged greeting party descended upon them.

A herd of Sika deer made their presence known. Normally a polite bow would do. However, the sniffing interest today seemed to be a whim for a possible catch brought in from the sea. Unfortunately, as they snooped through the humans' salt air-swept clothing, nothing of the like could be found. They postured to sit and gazed out to the waters as if waiting for the next beaching of travelers. Nonetheless, they appreciated the attention and patting.

Kami and JR found a seaside villa that met their needs. After settling in they proceeded down the beach to discover the tide was receding. They could now walk out to the vermillion structure and observe its massive reinforced base. Conches and crustaceans were embedded onto its foundation, clamping securely in between tides. It was a picturesque scene of orange against blue sky interrupted by a long shadow from the sun.

The Shinto Itsukushima shrine appeared behind the travelers, inviting them into a welcoming sanctuary. They viewed a ritual being performed for a young couple. A priest was waving a branch tied with lightning-shaped strips of paper over each of their shoulders. In the end, he tore off one strip of paper and gave it to the couple. Curiously, Kami took JR's hand and approached the shrine. She tossed a coin into the slotted wooden box. The priest gestured them in to sit on their knees and bow their heads. He took the branch with paper strips and waved it over their shoulders. He said a prayer. He then motioned for them to stand. He tore an end strip of the paper off the branch and handed it to them. He said, "You are now purified." All three bowed and stepped away. Kami opened the folded paper before JR. A commemorative seal of the shrine with the tori backdrop was stamped on it.

It was a short hike to the top of the island. The summit was called Misen. Unsurprisingly, it meant "moving materials." There, the couple sat quietly within the slope-roofed overhead shelter. It was unique in design. The angles from the eaves directed one's view. To the north were islands within the sea of Seto framed by an inlet which sheltered the shrine and grand gate. To the east, the sun transformed the water into a mist as it climbed into the virgin forest. To the west, varietal vegetation and fertile lands feasted on the rain and sun. Finally, to the south, unearthed mountain rocks dwelled in a place obscuring something sacred. A light rain tapped on the shelter's top eave and latticework. The vast space hypnotized them. They sat and observed the kaleidoscope of ever-changing nature.

After the sun had set, they made their way down to the villa. They entered the ryokan through the onslaught of konnichiwas from the staff. They turned to go to their room when they heard from a counter, "A cold one?" They knew the voice. They stepped over to the bar to join their new acquaintances, Kami spontaneously blurting, "Bloody ya, no drama, eh?" They raised the frothy and toasted, "Kanpai!" They downed them whole. Then Kami and JR smiled at each other and excused themselves for the evening. As they walked away, Michael shouted out, "Dive tomo?" JR replied, "Dive tomo!" with no idea what was meant.

They enjoyed a serene sunrise walk along the beach. The crimson hue of the sun colored with sea vapor ascended up the forested mountain, transforming into an undulating web of mist. They took biscuits with them to nourish the entourage of four-legged friends who happily greeted them. The quiet morning invited them to sit and contemplate on the sand. The gentle roll of high-tide waves lifted the shoreline. A tall shadow fell over them suddenly, yielding cause to lift their eyelids. The silence broke with a "G'day, mates!" The familiar voice continued, "Joining us for the dive?" JR uttered his own version of "Straya" slang: "Don't catch your drift?" Michael continued, "Well, mate, the conditions are tasty for a deep dip into the bay for some floor scruffy and sucker spearing." JR and Kami were intrigued but had difficulty with the onslaught of jargon. Nanette stepped forward to clarify.

"He means about a hundred feet out, the oysters are ready and octopus catching is ideal for a deep dive today." She followed, "Care to join us? We are getting ready." No longer distressed, JR and Kami looked at each other and nodded heads. Michael chimed, "Cheerio!"

In Japan, deep diving was a long established livelihood in providing seafood consumptives to families and locals. A wet suit, goggles, gloves, rock belt, basket, and extra-long flippers were essential. A spear was seldom used but generally sported by outsiders such as themselves. Nanette instructed, "You put on the wet suit, flippers, goggles, and rock belt. The flippers are especially long to give you speed in kicking to the bottom. The rock belt helps weigh you down. Afterwards, you toss the rocks off to ascend. The basket is floated at the top so you know where you are and have a deposit for the catch." She paused. "Michael will demonstrate."

Michael swam out about a hundred feet. He then tied a rock with a line to the basket which bobbed on the surface. He adjusted his goggles and gloves. He signaled to the others at shoreline. He curled into a forward ball and then extended down with flippers rising vertically out of water like a dolphin's tail. He vanished into the deep. No bubbles. No stir. Silence remained on the shore.

Time is a funny thing. In water, a minute can feel like ten. To JR that day, it seemed like an hour. For the three above the water's surface, the only reassurance was that they saw no bubbles. When the waiting seemed unbearable, much less the thought of actually holding one's breath for so long, a voice of reason reassured.

"Three minutes," said Nanette. "He'll be coming up now."

Michael surfaced next to the basket with a big exhale. His forearms, hands to elbows, were full of swirling tentacles. He reached over to deposit the slimy catch into the basket and kicked back to shore. Michael stood and grinned, "Fresh sucker for the barbie tonight!"

"Well, let's have a go at it!" he exclaimed to JR and Kami. He grabbed two spear guns. They all swam out to the location and grouped together their baskets. Michael handed a spear gun to JR, who winced. "Not for me." Michael then offered it to Kami. To her husband's surprise, she took it. They all donned masks and gloves and checked their belts. Nanette urged, "It's not that deep. We are together. Big breath. Get to the bottom and relax." All gave the thumbs-up. They dove.

She was right. The descent to the seabed came quickly and with minor effort. The meditation of the moment entered the stillness and they began to turn over treasures below. It became easy to lose track of time relishing the underwater nature of things. The snails, squid, and bottom feeders scurried away in surprise from grasping hands. Some tried to hold their ground in hope to scare the peddlers off. JR turned over a rock infested with moss. "Behold," he thought.

It was a giant oyster.

JR was hypnotized, floating above a seabed of discovery and life. Suddenly, Nanette tapped him and pointed to the top. He floated to the top by releasing his rocks and slung the heavy water-logged oyster into his basket. Nanette followed with handfuls of jumbo shrimp.

Unexpectedly, Michael surfaced exasperated, holding onto Kami. He exclaimed, "She speared a blue finner! We are going to have to beach it."

Holding onto the baskets, they swam as fast as they could to the shoreline. Michael let out all as much as he could of the spear line. They stood in the shallows with great anticipation. JR asked, "What's a blue finner?" Still rankled, Michael answered, "My god, bloke, it's a monster tuna! Now grab hold of the line and help me pull it in!"

The silvery side of the fish glistened against the sun as it surfaced with a pointed barb hunkered through its top back. Locals gathered around to help heave an additional line to shore past the surf. The effort was unwieldy and punishing for the arms and back. Michael sounded, "Heave-ho!" to aid the coordinated exertion. When they got the fish to the edge of the sand, they could pull no further. The tuna had grooved into the beach shallows. A small pickup truck appeared with back gate down. They tied ropes to the tail and fins. It took JR, Michael, and four Japanese men to hoist it onto the back gate and slide it in. The tail stuck out the back.

They got to the tori. There on the high crossbeam they could throw a line up and around. They pulled the truck underneath. All present took hold of the rope and hoisted the grand fish by its tail off the truck bed. They could only lift it so high that it barely had clearance from the ground. Then the locals lifted Kami next to it in an amusing, imposing display. It was twice the width and length of her. Michael strayed next to JR and uttered, "Little god slays big god."

One would wonder what to do with a fish that weighs over six hundred pounds. However, the islanders wasted no time to work. A table was set up. Laid out were heavy silk lace satchels. Inside were assorted steel single-edged honed knives.

The Japanese were well known for their skills in taking a piece of metal and forging it into a sword. The high-temperature flaming of select steel and coordinated rhythmic pounding into a flawless edge could only be mastered through time. A samurai's household would be praised when he could swipe the entire length of the blade through a torso. It was the dignified seal on a blade that protected the family. For the samurai, it was the required honor in battle. A thousand years of trade with China brought the acquired technique to their shores. The Japanese perfected it. After World War II, Conqueror MacArthur banned the production and possession of such katana. As a result, the instruction of sword skills by master to apprentice morphed into that of knife crafting. The handles of such were designed for ergonomic prehension. The evolved harmony of mastering the knife would be judged only by the designer's final culinary display.

With coordinated precision, the men started below the massive head and began slicing through the flesh. Large chunks were laid on the table. There, the portions were groomed into steaks and smaller fillets. Children would gather to watch as paper-thin pieces were handed out as sashimi to eat. After every cut, the knives were wiped in cloth and water for the continued assault. Any piece disturbed with a jagged edge or distracted slice was fed back into the sea.

JR went back to gather the remaining baskets from the dive. He remembered his find. He searched through the baskets. He reached down to pull out the oyster. He tried to open it but required an edge. He walked over to the table and placed it on top. Michael coughed and spoke, "Ya know, mate, I know what ya thinking. Stacks against you are 1 in 10,000 ya find one." Resolutely JR motioned to the Japanese to wedge in two knives. He pried as hard as he could. The mouth cleanly split open.

Oysters contain an internal organ known as the mantle. It gathers minerals from its food in a coat. In time, layers upon layers form and burnish the grain slowly to fashion the iridescent pearl.

JR looked and reached inside. He turned the oyster upside down into the cup of his right hand. He grasped inside and could feel the smooth roundness of a gem. He reached for Kami's hand and placed it between his. He now understood the symbolism and reality of Matthew 13. The revelation was clear to him.

The honeymooners prepared the kayaks for the trip back. They had only one more step to the west before their journey's end. The locals praised them for the gift from the sea. JR and Kami bowed in return. The Aussies hugged them. They began the paddle way out to the tori gate and stopped before passing through. They briefly paused to rest quietly under the massive beam. They did not say a word, nor did they look back. They knew the others would be watching from the shoreline. They could feel the magnetism pulling on their backs.

The crossing over was the hardest thing to do. It became too much, and they treaded water without forward motion. Finally, JR expressed to Kami a reflective maxim borrowed from his mother: "Come when you're needed, but go when you're wanted." It sounded good, but was still so difficult. They did not look back. They paddled on.

They made it back to the ferry docks and returned the kayaks. The rental car waited for them. It was then JR realized how challenging left-sided driving was. The great effort to follow the road lines opposite to his intuition exhausted him as well as Kami for being on constant lookout. He turned in his keys at the nearest rental location. A train station was within sight. A shiny bullet Shinkansen waited. They got on to reach their final end point.

Kokura would resonate the most for JR in Japan. He had carried this place in his psyche since boyhood. He had listened and learned of the great service of his father's duty there. A bridge formed to reach between their destinies at this moment in time. Kokura was destined to become the common ground where their two paths would cross.

XXXI

They pulled into Kokura station. It was not at all what he had expected. The developing city linked into the terminal of shops with modern buildings. He withdrew his only picture of TJ and the Navajo code talker from his wallet. The men were grinning in front of a handwritten city sign with a grand edifice to be seen in the distance behind. Now, he stepped from the terminal under a colossal bright sign flashing *Kokura* from above. Despite the urban progress, he attempted to envision and step back into TJ's time. It was where his father had walked thirty years ago. He had come to meet his past here.

They met a tour group of elders giving out historical information. He posed a question to them: "Did you see the Marines here during the war?" "Yes," replied the guides. "We do remember the Marines coming here. They helped rebuild our city. JR went on, "Can you point us to the castle?" They collectively pointed to a riverwalk.

Clouds began to gather and a light rain began to fall. JR and Kami covered their heads and walked across a long bridge broken up by a sculpture in the middle. A unique bronze figure of a man releasing doves into the sky was displayed. As they reached the far bank, they realized the significance of the bridge they were on. It would have been ground zero for the city. Spared atomic destruction due to such weather as this, Kokura had been given its second chance.

They entered a magnificently sculpted garden. Instantly, they could feel a space of tranquility and harmony. Laid stone steps all around led to evergreens, koi ponds, and lanterns. They stumbled upon a gathering of colorfully robed men holding long bows. They were archers. The scene harkened an earlier time and activity. Each practiced artful positions in drawing and taking aim at a diamond-shaped bull's-eye. The artistic chi likened to a mindfulness exercise of movement and consciousness more than of sport. The footwork, longbow draw, and slow-tempered release were maneuvered to score a target meters away. A young ceremonial man approached the couple in interest. He nodded politely then informed them, "This event comes from ancient times." He continued, "It displays the combination of militaristic skill and moving art form." JR spoke up. "It looks like an interesting form of archery?" The young man replied, "It is ancient archery. It is called the way of the bow." He then excused himself to partake in the activities.

Rising from the grounds sat the castle of Kokura. There was little foot traffic before the entrance. A slender elderly man with wire-rimmed glasses approached them with an identification badge. *Konnichiwa*s were exchanged. The man then stated, "I will be your guide forward. You look upon a sacred castle. It has been standing since the 1600s. It has escaped many military strikes." He continued, "The history of feudalism is told here. Let us climb to the top and I will explain more." He bowed and put out his hand that they should follow. JR and Kami nodded and accepted.

He spoke as they ascended the steps. "The Japanese feudal period lasted seven hundred years, up to 1900. That is why this castle exists." He went on, "It was a time of powerful families. In fact, one of which I come from. The emperor was merely a figurehead then. The military power came from the warlords called shoguns who divided the land according to class. The warriors, or samurai, kept the order and rule of Japan. Often, they were mere farmers. They followed strict codes and ethics." JR asked, "What about the common people?" The guide responded, "They were next in line. The efforts of all working class were required to build a castle. It stood to defend and protect the ruling families and display military might. The castle's great presence thwarted invaders from attack and gave further warning to outsiders."

They made it to the top floor. JR exclaimed, "Boy, what a view from all sides." He continued, "It would be difficult to not be seen from afar." Kami said to the man, "You said you came from a family that built such castles." "Yes," he replied. "I was close to being from samurai." He sighed. "But my ancestry took another path." Kami's curiosity took hold. "Please explain?" The man went on.

"The samurai believe and adhere to the seven ways. They are bushido, rectitude, courage, benevolence, politeness, veracity, and honor. They serve at that level." Kami broke in, "So what level did your ancestry serve at?" He hesitated and answered, almost embarrassedly, "We served at the level of ninja."

It was known that the ninja served with the lower classes next to the merchants in the feudal system. The merchant class was involved in dealing and arranging goods for money exchanges, often to their own benefit. The ninja did not live by the bushido of the samurai. Their methods and training were irregular at best. They were best known for covert and mercenary works which often led to sabotage, espionage, and even infiltration. Assassinations were not out of the question. They mastered weaponry, including flying daggers, iron hooks, spiked chains, and poisonous projectile stars, to name a few.

The ninja modus operandi revolved around secrecy. They would often blend in with the commoners for undercover methods of concealment and escape. Mostly, their dark ways would be obscured in monetary payment. It shadowed any sense of honor and glory.

The man spoke again, "I was a secret agent during the great war. I was captured. Even though I was used as an interpreter, I was still able to thwart efforts to collect information."

JR interrupted. "Were you an interpreter in nearby Sasebo?"

"Why, yes."

JR continued, "Do you remember a lieutenant? A Lieutenant TJ?"

The man took off his glasses and cleaned them carefully. "I only recall an officer in charge of the prison and church building."

JR stood silent for a moment. Kami then spoke up. "Do you remember an American interpreter by the name of Yaz?"

"Oh," he spoke. "I cannot forget. He traveled off with the most beautiful young woman here."

Kami pressed with greater interest, "Do you remember her name?"

"I believe it was Aya." He continued, "In fact, you remind me of her."

With glaring interest, Kami insisted, "Can you show me where they lived?"

He pointed out from the open window. "There. Down from that brass building." Kami and JR quickened their steps to the stairs. "Wait!" resounded the man. "This information does cost something." JR returned to give him some yen. He placed his glasses back on, looked at the yen, and stuffed it in his top pocket. He uttered, "If I can be of any further service in your stay, my name is Takamatsu." JR turned away replying, "Of course, I know your class!"

They raced back down the stairs. Then they walked down a street of apartments in a tenement setting, eyes perked. Kami remarked, "I hope someone around here remembers her."

JR suggested, "Do we just call out 'Aya' as we stroll?"

"No," said Kami, "We say 'Ayako.' Let us start in the brass shop." When they reached it a man came to the door. Kami started speaking in broken Japanese. "Mita me Ayako?"

A well-dressed middle-aged man got up from his desk further into the shop. "Can I help you?" he said.

"Thank you. I am looking for the home of Ayako who once lived in this area years ago."

He motioned to step outside. "I remember Aya. However, very few inquire about an Ayako." He hesitated, "Why do you ask?"

"She is my mother," Kami stated.

He paused at length and replied, "And I am her brother."

They looked at each other in astonishment.

He continued, "I lost contact with her when she left so long ago. But we were raised in the same tenement." He sighed and went on, "During the war our parents took up the duty to fight for the emperor and Japan. During that away time, they appointed a designated guardian as our caregiver. They were gone so long it seemed as if they would never return. In that time, Aya vowed to protect and take care of me wherever the future might hold. But then came the American repatriation. She met a Native American marine private and they fell in love. He promised her a new life and beginning in America. She wanted me to go with them. However, my pride was too great for Japan. I wanted to stay here and commit myself to the skills of a brasserie apprentice. Just before she left for America, Aya added my name, Ko, to the end of hers to remember me in whatever she did and wherever she would go. Suddenly, shortly after this, my father returned but with the news of my mother's passing near the sacred grounds of Mount Daisen. With Aya in America, he could not bear to stay here and returned to the revered mountains to be near my mother's spirit thereafter."

Kami reached out to him and embraced him. She said, "So your name is Ko?"

"Yes," he replied.

"And I am Kami. My mother is known as Dr. Ayako in

Tokyo. I know she would be so proud of you. She uses her name with honor for all to hear and see."

Unexpectedly, JR stepped forward to introduce himself as well. He followed, "My father, also, was an American officer here during the war."

Ko broke in, "I do recall an officer, a lieutenant, in the company of the private. He had a single-star Jeep I liked. I once took him and the private around in a rickshaw. He introduced me to baseball!" Suddenly, Ko realized what he was saying and exclaimed, "You mean, that lieutenant was your father! And that private was *your* father!!" He looked from JR to Kami. He went on, "I must take you to what the Americans did here. Wait just a moment." He grabbed a set of keys and had them jump into his car. They drove along the oceanside to a bay of docked boats.

JR noticed on the dashboard a baseball with *Tokyo Giants* inscribed on its surface and other baseball paraphernalia throughout the car. JR asked, "Did you play?"

Ko replied, "I did. I learned quickly. I was a good hitter and outfielder for the Giants." He continued, "It was at a time where I was very young and I could run and hit better than anyone." He continued, "What you see is the last baseball I hit to save a game. It was the team's gift to me."

They entered the city of Sasebo. "Look!" He pointed. "That is the church your father came to build." The view was obscured by mist and surrounding buildings. "I will take you in. It is a very sacred place." JR responded, "Oh, I believe it." Ko responded, "No, it is more than you expect." They made a turn into the harbor area and parked. "We must walk in from here," said Ko.

They walked down a stone pathway. JR slipped his hand into Kami's. The familiar sight of a vermillion tori gate was ahead. They bowed as they passed through. An amphitheater of harmoniously shaped structures came into view.

To the left stood a five-level pagoda with curved copper roofing and open sills. Incense burned at the entrance. Next to it, a temple displayed a domed top. The open-air design invited the travelers to sit before the Bodhisattva.

To the right was a Shinto shrine with altar stones, a ceremonial hanging straw bale, and a bell. Then, a statue of the Virgin Mary in a grotto with interconnected bridges over a pond of koi, lotus, chrysanthemums, evergreens, and roses leading multiple paths toward her. Last, a stone cathedral displaying twelve standing disciple orifices. It had a simple cedar door and a crucifix on top. They walked up to the middle hub of the intersecting paths. They looked down to see a particular stone embedded in the ground calling notice. Engraved on it was an epithet that read:

To the brave Americans who helped us build this sacred place.

JR walked into the church and knelt. It was pure emotion for him. He did not know how to contain himself. He just wept. He had journeyed far, just as his father had. Somehow, all of it made sense in this place of ancestry. It was all connected.

Finally he stood up to exit and opened the doors. Kami was seen to the side. She was in front of Mary. He approached her and watched. She presented a small cedar plaque painting of two ceremonially dressed men holding bells and chimes in a dance around one another.

She spoke in front of Our Lady the words, "To the transformation of two great souls meeting." She then placed it at her feet.

XXXII

They returned to Ko's brasserie. JR bought a brass toy Jeep from Ko. They would have liked more time to spend. Well-wishes were in order. Ko mentioned that he hoped to see Aya again. Kami expressed, "No worries. I am certain she'll be back."

They had traveled far. Even by Shinkansen speed, it took them the whole day to return to Tokyo. It was late when they pulled into Tokyo station. They could see now why the capsule hotels were so popular, especially after distance traveling. They welcomed the convenience and relief.

The next morning they darted to Tsuji Market for fresh fish. JR compared Kami's grand catch to the display of junior tuna. During breakfast, they caught wind of a spectacular outlook of the city from a tower. Enthusiastically, they took the metro to Roppongi stop for a dash up the Mori Tower. At the top was a panoramic view of Tokyo and the distant Mount Fuji. It was breathtaking.

They noticed a photographer taking pictures. A dapper European-looking man with a slicked mustache was frantically snapping away at the plethora of visuals. He requested to take a photo of them. JR obliged. He then asked JR for a picture of Kami alone. JR responded, "Make it good. Just one." He instructed her in a look-away pose against the Bay of Tokyo toward the Meiji shrine. *Click.*

JR inquired, "What are you going to use it for?" The photographer replied in broken English, "Perdon, I use da photo for da magazine. Maybe I use a this a one for da cover." JR went on, "Where will it be published?" "Maybe da America!" he grinned. "Where elsa ya find da Statue of Libertia." The man then smiled and politely excused himself.

They returned to the ryokan. Waiting was a message with a return phone number. It was from Dr. Isao. It read, *Foundation updates. Please contact me as soon as you can.* JR immediately phoned. Isao updated him, "Nice to hear from you. I hope your travels went well. We have some news. The foundation needs your help. We have relocated many patients from Saigon to Tokyo. We also have been informed that you need to report to the U.S. embassy." Kami gently pulled on JR's shirt to speak to Isao as well. She asked, "Is Ayako here?" "Yes, with Reiko," he responded and continued, "I must go now. Please check in with us tomorrow. Arigato."

They arrived at the hospital the next day. They walked into the dedicated floor to see rows and rows of children. Reiko and Ayako spotted them off to the side. "Konnichiwa!" they exclaimed, "So happy to see you!" Instinctively, they embraced each other. Ayako said, "We heard your travels were adventurous and grand. My father called. He enjoyed your visit." The couple responded, "Likewise!"

Reiko continued, "We have much to tell you. The foundation has moved many of the children here for rehabilitation care." She continued, "We have them intermixed with Japanese children so they can learn new ways to communicate and help each other. The foundation believes in cultural integration so that we as one large family can succeed. Of course, you two understand all this." The married couple smiled. "Well, where do we start?" asked JR. "We have you with our children amputees. That is your specialty. You can help bridge the needs. For one in particular." She finished with a smile and excused herself.

They made their way toward the children's group. Instantly, one female Japanese child stood out. She was instructing the other children in English. They sat to observe. After this, the girl prompted the children into dancing lessons on their prosthetic legs. Finally, she broke out into a song.

She sang the song of peace. Kami and JR recognized the melody from before the ceremonial dove release in Hiroshima. They continued to observe and listen. The child sang at the top of her voice and gestured these words with her hands:

> This is my song
> Oh god of all the nations
> A song of peace for lands so far away
> This is my home, a country where my heart is
>
> But other hearts in other lands are beating
> With hopes and dreams as true and high as mine
> O hear my prayer, o god of all nations
> A song of peace for their lands and for mine.

Happy clapping ensued. She then helped the children with prostheses to stand and sway with her to the melody again. Afterward, she had them sit. Finally, she promptly served them tea. Ayako was also watching the scene from the back. She came over to Kami and JR and asked, "You have met her?"

"No," they replied. "She is remarkable."

Ayako revealed, "The only home she knows is this one. She was given to us and we have made a place for her. She knows no parents."

JR replied, "We must have an introduction!" Kami and JR went up to the girl and bowed. JR began, "What is your name?"

She replied, "My name is Roren."

JR followed, "Ah, you are a great lion in our midst."

Roren laughed and then bowed humbly. She asked, "Do you like my job and my story?"

"Very much!"

Roren went on, "I have heard very much about you two. Dr. Ayako and Dr. Reiko have told me. You have traveled far with many questions." She paused. "I hope I am one of your answers."

JR and Kami asked Roren if she would have time for lunch in her busy schedule caring for the other children. She checked. "Why, yes!" In the meantime, they worked together. They checked children's limbs for the fitting of the variety of prostheses available.

At noon, they walked out to a courtyard with provided bento boxes. Roren said, "Inside is my favorite rice. It is white." Kami responded, "Is it ever any other color?" The girl stated, "Sometimes it is brown or black! It all tastes the same. But, I like white!" They laughed. JR noticed a slight limp in her step and her foot turned slightly out. JR spoke, "Let me fix that for you." She sat on a step while JR slid off her prosthetic leg and re-donned it for better positioning. "How did you know?" Roren asked, surprised. JR smiled and replied, "Let's just say I have been watching people walk for a while."

She then explained, "I was born without a leg. I guess I was incomplete to my parents. They say I was found in front of this hospital. It was Dr. Reiko who picked me up and gave me my special room. Would you like to see it?"

"Sure," they said.

They climbed up a set of stairs in the hospital to a corner room. It looked like a storage space. She opened the door. It had a futon and a window facing out to a park. On the walls were drawings of places. She pointed and explained, "That's me on the

Golden Gate Bridge in San Francisco. This one's me on top of the Empire State Building. And that's me sliding down the Arch in St. Louis!"

"Wow," they remarked. "These drawings are so good. Have you been to these places?" "No," she replied, "except in my dreams." Suddenly she said, "Oh, we must get back. We must not waste time!" JR responded, "Yes, that is all we have."

They returned to the clinic. Kami and JR sat quietly to ponder. They asked Reiko for the afternoon off. The couple walked to the familiar St. Ignatius grounds. They entered and kneeled inside to pray. Then they exited to sit in the garden and meditate. They stayed there for some time. Then JR moved to sit in front of Kami and held her hands. JR spoke freely. "Roren has shown us her walk. Are we being asked to show her a part of our walk?" Kami smiled brightly and embraced her husband.

Afterwards they met up with Ayako and Reiko sitting at a table. JR looked at Kami and began, "We would like to give Roren a new home. Her soul and spirit has touched ours." He went on, "If it possible, we would like your permission to do so." Ayako spoke, "You mean to adopt Roren?" "Yes", said Kami. Reiko spoke, "I was waiting for this day and for this moment. This is why you have reached so far." She continued, "You can start immediately on the procedures. I knew you three were a match!" Ecstatically they hugged each other. "Wait," said JR. "We need to tell her." Ayako spoke and smiled confidently. "Trust in my wisdom as a mother: She already knows."

Adoption in Japan is very unique. International procedures have little standards except in the political process. A sponsor is required. A week's stay is all that is required for legal guardianship. Beyond that, the adoption is then finalized in America.

The couple approached Fr. Raphael in church. He was glad to see them again. He had heard they were back. He happily greeted them. "So happy you two found each other. And now there is a third." JR remarked, "Word travels quick here." "Yes," he said and cited, "Like the Holy Family." JR mentioned, "We need a sponsor to help us expedite our family. Could you be of help?" Fr. Raphael replied, "Leave it to me. Come back here tomorrow afternoon."

Since it was late in the day, they returned to the ryokan. A message was waiting for them. It read, *Please contact the U.S. embassy.* JR phoned and was told, "Your deployment is up. We require you to return to the United States for an official discharge of duties." JR looked at Kami. He stated, "We have to act quickly."

They met with Fr. Raphael and another priest the following day. The latter introduced himself, "I am Fr. Santos. Fr. Raphael has spoken highly of you two." He went on, "I am a Trappist monk and represent Faith International. I hear you wish to adopt a child?" JR responded, "Yes, Father." He continued, "We know we may or may not have our own. That is not for us to decide. We know children are a gift. We are asked to be good stewards of this gift." Fr. Santos nodded and followed, "Most importantly, are you doing this out of love?" Kami replied, "Most importantly, yes."

Faith International became their sponsor and began the paperwork. JR took a moment to his own solitude. He decided to write to his parents. Then he thought better of it, gesturing to Kami, "No, I need to call my parents. Come share the news with me." They spent the rest of the afternoon into the evening speaking with TJ and Helen. Many stories were shared and the many unforeseen coincidences of their mutual journeys were relayed. The coming-together story of new family was not to be delivered in short form. After all, there was much to be said for this far reach.

With the added help of Isao, Reiko, and Ayako, the embassy approved the request for the couple's return to the United States with Roren. Ayako spoke, "We will miss our talented and adventurous friends." Reiko followed, "We must go now. We have much to do." Isao conveyed to JR, "I am glad your adventure in Japan went well. It is very special. And your Roren is beautiful."

He continued, "Maybe someday I will adventure to see your America." He then handed them airline tickets in a token of their appreciation. "Until then, sayonara, my friends!" JR replied, "Thank you, and much success to all your efforts here." He and Kami bowed and watched as they walked away. Unexpectedly, JR summoned Isao's ear with a loud call: "Remember, the kanto sword awaits its warrior!"

XXXIII

They caught the early flight. As the plane banked around the Tokyo metropolis, JR kept his eyes glued to the city from his window seat. He pondered the events he had encountered about the country and the journey he and his father shared. Out of the corner of his eye, he caught a glimpse of a remarkable sight. In disbelief, he saw the glimmer of the Statue of Liberty just off the entrance to the bay. Indeed, democracy gleamed in the sunrise of this distant land. He then remembered what the photographer had said. He looked for his card in his pockets, but somehow he had misplaced it. He sighed. Nonetheless, America had left its mark on the next renaissance of Japan. JR stretched to look back and said fondly, "Sayonara."

Los Angeles was fifteen hours away. In that time, Kami and JR shared their feelings of how country and duty touched their lives. Roren drew a vision of a new, distant home. Each of them born in one country but drawn to another by destiny. After a while, they could see the long-awaited coastline of California. They had traveled through time zones and the international dateline, placing them into the airport a day prior to takeoff. They quickly changed into their commemorative uniforms, hoping they would serve well in expediting through the lines. Customs was welcoming.

It was a short layover at LAX. They had time to stretch and walk the terminal. Kami and Roren, with hands entwined, danced on the wide floors of the terminal. JR got the coffees. The girls gleamed when JR brought Kami a matcha mocha and Roren a strawberry shake.

They made their way over to the bookstands. As they perused the materials, suddenly Roren exclaimed to Kami, "Look, Mommy, it's your picture!" Kami looked and her jaw dropped. She handed a publication to JR. A picture of her overlooking Tokyo from a great height was front and center. He looked close to see the name of the magazine. JR remarked, "Oh my gosh, *Condé Nast.*" The title read, *Open your Horizons.* JR bought out all the issues.

They boarded for the last leg of the trip. They still had four hours of flying time to Milwaukee. He realized that the six thousand plus miles was not an easy draw. The Midwest greenery started to come into view as the growing plethora of lakes mirrored off the wing of the plane. They banked around the Great Lake of Michigan just outside of Chicago in the descent. Roren exclaimed, "Oh good, another sea!"

They landed at Mitchell Field with great anticipation. So much went through JR's head. So much went through Kami's. What would the meeting be like for all? What would it look like? What would the first impression be?

They exited the plane and stepped onto the tarmac. Kami and JR walked behind Roren. They kissed each other, took a deep breath, and walked into the terminal. Ahead JR could see an unmistakable figure at attention reflecting "semper fi." JR raised his hand to reach his notice. He returned the gesture. It was TJ. The family gathered and surrounded them in embrace for this long-awaited homecoming.

JR expressed, "We have so much to share in our family." Without notice, Roren stepped up to her grandfather announcing, "Konnichiwa, welcome home!" TJ crouched to his knees to look in her eyes. He replied, "Konnichiwa, welcome home."